THE STONE CROSS

Published for the Stefanyk Centennial Committee
by McClelland & Stewart Limited

Translated from the Ukrainian by Joseph Wiznuk in
collaboration with C. H. Andrusyshen

VASYL STEFANYK
THE STONE CROSS

The Canadian Publishers
McClelland and Stewart Limited
25 Hollinger Road, Toronto 374

Printed and bound in Canada by
John Deyell Limited

Contents

Acknowledgements

On behalf of the Stefanyk Centennial Committee, we wish to extend our very sincere thanks to all those who made it financially posible to publish these stories by Vasyl Stefanyk.

We should like to thank Professor C. H. Andrusyshen for his collaboration with the Reverend Joseph Wiznuk in the translation of these stories. Rev. Wiznuk translated twenty-two stories; Professor Andrusyshen translated ten, corrected and edited all translations, and prepared all of the stories for publication.

We extend our thanks also to Mrs. Sophia Temnycka in Newark, N.J., who collected a substantial sum of money for this purpose; to Mr. James G. MacGregor in Edmonton for his assistance; and to Mr. Stanley W. Frolick, Q.C., in Toronto, for arranging the publication of these selected works and liaison between this Committee and the publishing house of McClelland and Stewart Limited.

Without the help of these persons we would not have been able to have published the stories of our famous writer, Vasyl Stefanyk, on the occasion of the 100th anniversary of his birth, which will be celebrated in 1971.

For the Stefanyk Centennial Committee:

T. Kobzey, Chairman
Dr. B. Martynovych, Vice-Chairman
M. Worobec, Secretary

The publication of this book was made possible by a grant from the Taras Shevchenko Foundation, the support of the Ukrainian Reading Association, Prosvita, in Winnipeg, and by individual donors through the Stefanyk Centennial Committee in Winnipeg.

Preface

This is not the first time Vasyl Stefanyk's stories have been translated into English. Since 1920, many have appeared in various Canadian, American and English newspapers and journals, most of them rendered by Dr. C. H. Andrusyshen. By now, however, quite a number of those miniature masterpieces, while still existing in the files of the editorial offices, are almost inaccessible to the general reading public. It was therefore considered imperative to have a selection of Stefanyk's stories translated and published in a permanent book form, particularly since the hundredth anniversary of his birth is to be celebrated throughout the Slavic world in 1971. In this way those responsible for the collection intend to pay homage to this great man whose artistic product deserves world-wide recognition.

For this purpose a special publication committee, under the headship of Mr. Toma Kobzey, was formed, and the translation was initially entrusted to the Rev. Joseph Wiznuk, who was the first to bear the brunt of the immense difficulties encountered en masse in Stefanyk's involved style and idiomatic manner of writing. Well-versed in Ukrainian and English, Mr. Wiznuk, who has been toying since his youth with Stefanyk's works, admirably managed to translate twenty-two stories. However, Stefanyk's highly idiomatic and complex style and his use of dialect required such exactitude that the committee thought it advisable to invite Dr. C. H. Andrusyshen to review the translations, edit and polish them to the best of his ability, and so produce a new version of the selections. In the process he increased the collection by ten more pieces which bear his initials. For these he alone is responsible. It must be emphasized that his alterations of Mr. Wiznuk's performance do not in the least detract from the latter's effort to accomplish excellent renditions of Stefanyk's works. Yet it must be firmly borne in mind that the author's diction is so condensed and replete with impressionistic and even hyperbolic phrases and passages that another scholar was needed to make the entire translation more precise, round out the meanings Stefanyk sought to convey, and so attain a result with which non-Ukrainian readers would be tolerably satisfied.

To achieve a translation acceptable to them, Professor C. H. Andrusyshen, after he had completed his work, considered it expedient to consult Dr. Howard German, Professor of English at the University of Saskatchewan. Having read the manuscript, the latter offered many useful suggestions which, for the greater part, were incorporated in this collection. His endeavor is here acknowledged with much gratitude. It must not, however, be assumed that he is liable for any limitations that may be found in this volume.

Without labouring this point too much, may it be repeated that Vasyl Stefanyk's style is so exceptional that at times it is impossible to translate him into another language. As a result, wherever such almost insurmountable hindrances occurred, both collaborators racked their brains to supply the closest approximations. In this translation the reader may often come across expressions with which he is not at all familiar, as in "The Trial" – "it came to such a pass that someone's life had to face death." Occasionally, when English phraseology appeared somewhat literal in transmission, the translators preferred its preservation rather than destroy the poetic value of the original. Let us hope that the risk they took may not prove too detrimental to English idiom. The reader must constantly remember that Vasyl Stefanyk is a literary giant with whom it is quite strenuous to grapple.

Although it may be going against present English and American practices, Dr. Andrusyshen thought it better to maintain Stefanyk's usage in having direct and indirect quotations preceded by a colon instead of a comma. This manner of punctuation may in time, let us hope, creep into the English system. Likewise it will be found that in "The Signature," where the speaker relates a conversation, a dash is placed before each quotation. Otherwise, the entire long passage would become too cluttered with apostrophies and quotation marks.

Certain Ukrainian words, such as "gazda," "kum," "pazukha," "prizba," and others used in the original, have no exact equivalents in English. The closest English synonym of "gazda" is "landholder," "proprietor," "squire." But the third meaning, although used in "May," cannot be correctly employed anywhere else. The word "kum" or "kuma" applies to "godfather" and "godmother" respectively. Where absolutely necessary, these English equivalents are used; otherwise, especially where clumsiness may result, the translators took the liberty of substituting such words as 'friend," "crony," "buddy," "chum," and other similar substantives. In so doing, they are to some degree justified, for, in the course of time, the meaning of "kum" and "kuma" has been extended to apply to "bosom (intimate) friend" or "boon companion," regardless of their original connotations. The most difficult of them all is perhaps "pazukha." It denotes the space inside the front part of a peasant's shirt where a fairly large pocket is formed, especially if the shirt is encircled above the waist by a sash or a cord. This word is rendered in several appropriate ways in the stories. The word "prizba" is always used as in the original, and its meaning is explained in the footnotes. Some of the footnotes may be found repetitious. In many instances this was done for the benefit of those who will prefer to read stories at random.

It is with grateful appreciation that the collaborators acknowledge the assistance they received from Mr. Toma Kobzey of Winnipeg, Manitoba, who is the Chairman of the Publication Committee consisting of himself, Dr. B. Martynovych, and Mr. M. Worobec. It was he, together with his colleagues, who was the motivating force that brought this publication to the light of day. Great indebtedness is likewise due to Mr. J. G. MacGregor, the author of the highly commendable and vital *Vilni Zemli,* recently published by McClelland and Stewart Limited, Toronto, and to Mr. S. W. Frolick, Q.C., for their keen interest in this work.

Special recognition is to be tendered to those organizations which contributed generously toward the material needs of the Stefanyk Publication Committee. Among them are The Ukrainian Canadian Committee, which, through its Shevchenko Foundation, donated $1,500, and the Reading Society, "Prosvita" ($500).

Nor should one forget those donors who, by their various material assistance, helped to cover the costs of this commemorative volume. Their kindness is accepted with a great feeling of obligation on the part of those who were actively engaged in what is hoped will be a work worthy of the greatness of Vasyl Stefanyk.

The Life and Work of
Vasyl Stefanyk (1871-1936)

Among world-renowned writers Vasyl Stefanyk has attained a place of enormous prominence in spite of his modest literary output. His collected miniatures – poems in prose and short stories – number but seventy-two and are regional in character; yet so great is their realistic and psychological impact that they prove Stefanyk equal in eminence to those whose creative endeavour consists of scores of volumes. *Homo unius libri,* as he might well be considered, his brief product is so concentrated that it, as often as not, surpasses that of authors whose eloquent verbiage requires years of comprehensive scrutiny.

He was born on May 14, 1871, in the village of Russiv – one of the most beautiful spots in the southwestern part of Ukraine, in Pokut'ya, neighbouring on the province of Bukovina. His father, Semen, was a wealthy landowner who increased his property by breeding cattle which he transported to Vienna where the price per head was much greater than on the local market. Semen married Oksana Keyvan when he was only eighteen. Vasyl was the second child of the family; the older by two years was Maria. Two more brothers and a sister followed. From his mother and Maria Vasyl received a love whose warmth he never forgot. They taught him not only to cherish the soil on which, as a child, he worked, but also old tales and songs that emerged from those who inhabited the district from time immemorial. Both his mother and sister later appeared in certain of his stories as prototypes of the solid type of peasantry who tilled the rich black soil of Pokut'ya. His relations with his father were only tepid, for Semen was a thorough materialist whose chief aim was to garner as much opulence as his expertness allowed during some forty years of his husbandry on the estate. To that end he exploited not only his hirelings but his own family, especially his wife whom he expected to attend to almost all the details of the household as well as to do fieldwork, as a result of which she became so exhausted that she died prematurely on January 1, 1900. It may be assumed that certain minor traits of his father were later incorporated in "The Arsonist," a story which the son wrote in the early part of his literary career.

The boy received his primary schooling in the nearby town of Sniatyn where he and the peasant students were treated with derision by the sons of the rich townsmen as well as by the teachers themselves. Having completed his studies there, he was sent to the Polish gymnasium at Kolomiya where, because of his lowly origin, he, and others like him, smarted under no less scorn. Among the indignities they endured was that of being advised to return to their villages to herd swine. However, the young students bore up under this persecution. In fact, they stood their ground and even organized themselves into a group whose main purposes were to enlighten the peasants in the surrounding communities by reading forbidden books to them and to arrange meetings at which the farm workers were encouraged to join the radical movement then spreading in Western Ukraine. The policies of the Radical Party at that time were not extreme; they only served to protect the interests of the destitute peasants against the extortions of the rich.

As a student, Stefanyk cared little for the kind of education he acquired from the gymnasium. In his words "the teaching was tedious, futile, empty." It was with great bitterness that he condemned this institution of supposedly higher learning, stating in no uncertain terms that, besides the ordinary instruction and a hostile attitude towards the Ukrainian students, it gave them very little. Being so neglected, they had to fend for themselves and gain the knowledge they needed from their own educational, social and political circles.

Stefanyk's literary activity began about this time. In collaboration with his friend, Les Martovych, who was later to become a celebrated writer himself, he wrote a few short stories; but actually his letters to his friends were his first exercises in belles lettres. It took him at least ten years before he overcame his timidity and began his career as a fully-fledged writer.

Before that happened, his radicalism led to his expulsion from the gymnasium at Kolomiya, and in 1890 he moved to the town of Drohobych to complete his advanced studies. This was Ivan Franko's territory, and it was in the village of Nahuyevychi, where Franko was born, that Stefanyk met this great poet and political leader. Their friendship lasted till the older writer's death in 1916.

His elation at contracting such a friendship was dampened by the news of his sister Maria's death. Shortly before Vasyl's matriculation, his father arrived at Drohobych to deliver this painful information. He spent three days with his son without daring to tell him what had occurred. Only when he boarded the train on the way home did he cry out: "Vasyl, Maria is dead." These sad tidings stunned Stefanyk, and he mourned the passing of his adored sister till the end of his days.

In 1892, at the insistence of his father, he went to Cracow to study medicine. There he remained till 1900 without completing the course. The fact of the matter was that he disliked medical studies, preferring his political interests and literary career. On many occasions, when visiting various villages in Western Ukraine, he called the attention of the authorities to the sorry lot of the peasantry. During the elections to the Galician *Soym* (Legislature) in 1895, he was arrested for his speeches on behalf of candidates who supported the Radical Party's programme, and spent two weeks in prison in Kolomiya. He likewise took part in the elections to the Austrian Parliament in 1897, for the most part under the cover of secrecy.

Finding his son's medical studies much too prolonged and his political zeal too excessive, Stefanyk's father became so exasperated that he discontinued material support. If it had not been for his mother, who supplied him with whatever he needed, Stefanyk would have found himself in straitened circumstances indeed.

While in Cracow, he became acquainted with many Ukrainian students with whom he continued his cultural and political development. Quite influential were his friendships with young Polish writers who introduced him to the modern literary trends then prevalent in Western Europe. Perhaps the greatest event that occurred to him was his meeting with Dr. Waclaw Moraczewski, who was married to the first woman doctor, a Ukrainian, in the Austrian Empire, Sophia Okunevska. His letters to them were of such great merit, some almost novelettes, that the distinguished chemist-doctor, who was also a connoisseur of world literature, at once began to encourage him to write. That was precisely what Stefanyk did.

So close was their friendship that Dr. Moraczewski not only served him as an advisor in many of his personal problems and assisted him materially, but also translated several of his stories into Polish and had them published in literary journals in which he likewise wrote favourable articles about Stefanyk's works. In his concise estimations of his closest friends, compiled under the title "The Heart," Stefanyk wrote that Dr. Moraczewski showed him the way into the world.

In one of his depressed moods, Stefanyk described his state of mind to his friend by citing Paul Verlaine (whose gloomy expres-

sion is rendered here in a somewhat paraphrastic manner):
"Silent sobbings. The damp autumn is weeping sadly. My heart
is seized with shudderings as savage despair plays upon it. I wander
about in pain in a painful world. I am all emaciated, as if
beaten down by the wind. On the barren fields I am but a withered
leaf."

Stefanyk needed consolation, and he got it from the Moraczew-
skis. In gratitude, he wrote them in 1897: "Before you came, I
could not find my place among people. But you did come, and the
world became lighter to me. Such a decisive influence did you have
on me that I found it much easier to live. My personal life is very
hard, but you have somehow changed it."

After a long epistolary schooling (one might call it his labora-
tory period), Stefanyk began to write his short stories. Most of his
symbolistic sketches which were classified as "poetry in prose,"
were written while he was on vacation in the town of Storozhyntsi,
Bukovina, at the home of Dr. Okunevska's father. These were not
too popular with Ukrainian publishers, and many were lost in
editorial offices. More important, however, were his short stories,
several of which he also wrote, or sketched, while on a visit at
Okunevsky's residence. The first story of his to be published was
"The Recruit's Farewell," which appeared in the newspaper
Pratsia, in Chernivtsi, towards the end of 1897. Also at the capital
of Bukovina, a collection of fifteen stories which bore the title of
the first, "The Blue Book," was printed in the spring of 1899.
Stefanyk was then twenty-eight years old.

Other collections followed in close succession: *The Stone Cross*
(Lviv, 1900), containing nine stories; *The Road* (Lviv, in the early
part of 1901), comprising thirteen items; and *My Word* (Lviv,
1905). This last collection included certain stories from *The Blue
Book* and *The Stone Cross*. Only two new works were added:
"The Trial" and "My Word," the latter an impressionistic auto-
biography. All of these stories were written not later than 1901,
when Stefanyk's first period of literary activity ended. For the next
fifteen years he remained silent as an author. Within three or four
years of intensive labour he had written forty-nine stories which
enriched Ukrainian literature immeasurably. Now he could turn
to other, less onerous pursuits.

However restricted this biography is, one cannot avoid men-
tioning a brief love episode in Stefanyk's life. In 1899, in the
parish of Triytsia, he met Yevhenia Kalytovska, the wife of the
local priest and the daughter of Kirilo Hamorak, likewise a priest,

serving in the prosperous village of Stetseva near Russiv. Stefanyk and she became seriously enamoured of each other and, for some time, remained in a quandary as to what they were to do. However, after considering that she was already married and the mother of two children, they concluded that a disruption of her marriage was unthinkable. To both the decision was a bitter one. Stefanyk's affection for her never ceased, and in his short registry of what his most important friends meant to him, "The Heart," he referred to her as "his greatest ideal of womanhood." The literary consequence of this affair were two impressionistic chefs-d'oeuvre, "Confiteor" (later renamed "My Word") and "The Road," both written to Yevhenia, in 1899 and 1900 respectively, as birthday gifts. These personal confessions, of course, were not intended for print, and he sent them to her sister, Olha, with whom he had been corresponding for many years and who later became his wife, to transmit to Yevhenia, who received them with heartache. Both sisters were extremely disturbed by the highly pessimistic tone in those lyrics in prose, and pleaded with him to abandon his hopeless yearning and seek his equanimity in rationality. Furthermore, they finally convinced him that, since no one would suspect to whom those masterly pieces were addressed, they should by all means be published. Reluctantly, he consented. In the end wisdom prevailed over passion.

These years were critical for Stefanyk. He underwent a series of crises which he found difficult to overcome. He was worried about the apathy of the peasant masses to the socialist appeal, and about the discord in the Radical Party itself. The death of his beloved mother, on the first day of the new century, left him prostrate. The abyss between himself and his father widened when the latter, after six months of mourning, remarried, much to the disapproval of the son. All these and other adversities caused a nervous breakdown that lasted several years. The intensity of his work on "Maple Leaves" and "The Arsonist" only worsened his condition. There was nothing for him to do but to leave Cracow and seek the renewal of his spiritual strength among his friends scattered throughout Western Ukraine.

Soon after regaining his emotional stability, in 1903, Stefanyk went to Kiev where he met such literary figures as M. Kotsiubinsky, Lesia Ukrainka, M. Staritsky and others. He also visited the town of Kaniv to pay homage to Taras Shevchenko. From the top of the great poet's mound he bowed his head in reverence to the entire Ukraine. From there he travelled to Poltava to be present at the unveiling of the monument to Ivan Kotliarevsky who, in 1798, with his comical travesty of Virgil's *Aeneid*, written in pure Ukrainian vernacular, initiated the modern trend in Ukrainian literature.

In January, 1904, when he was almost thirty-five, he married Olha Hamorak. They settled in her father's home in Stetseva where, with some success, he began to work the land. His father was overjoyed and prevailed on him to return to Russiv where he was given some fifteen acres of land to till. In March of 1910 Stefanyk returned to his native village, and there had a comfortable home built for himself and his family.

However, he never neglected his political mission among the peasantry; in the 1908 national elections to the Austrian Parliament, Dr. Volodymyr Okhrymovych was elected with Stefanyk as his alternate. Since the former refused to serve, Stefanyk became the deputy in the Federal House of Representatives and retained that post for ten years, until the downfall of the Austro-Hungarian Empire in 1918. He was not particularly pleased with himself during that period. Not once did he deliver a speech in Parliament; but, as a member, he was influential in assisting those who asked for his intervention. He was overwhelmed by countless petitions from his constituents whom he sought to satisfy in every way. Those who needed medical or legal help he would send to his professional friends who, in many cases, offered their services gratis. Other necessary work he performed himself. In spite of his serious manner and abrupt nature, at heart Stefanyk was a kindly man and never begrudged his time to those in need.

On February 4, 1916, Stefanyk's wife died, leaving him and his three sons, Semen, Kirilo, and Yurko, in great sorrow. At their mother's request, her sister, Olena Pleshkan, came to take care of the children and of the household, relieving the grieving father of much of the domestic burden.

A few months later the first World War broke out. The Tsarist army, among whom there were many Ukrainians, invaded Western Ukraine. After its retreat, on someone's denunciation, Stefanyk was arrested by the Austrian military command. Only his coolness and clever wit saved him from execution. During the second Russian invasion he fled to Vienna where he remained for a year, after which he returned to Russiv to be near his family and to resume writing after an interval of a decade and a half. The first story he wrote while yet in Vienna was "The Children's Adventure." In it were reflected his first impressions of the horrors of

9

the war. His fifth collection of stories appeared in Lviv in 1926, under the title *The Earth*. Its eight short pieces bear the imprint of the armed conflict and contain such novelettes as "Maria" and "The Sons." The remaining stories and études, which he wrote between 1926 and 1933, were included in the edition of his *Complete Works* which was published in the latter year in Lviv.

After the collapse of the Austro-Hungarian Empire, he was called to Lviv in the fall of 1918 as one of the former members of the Austrian Parliament but, after the Polish forces began to press hard against the troops of Western Ukrainian National Republic, which was proclaimed on November 1, 1918, Stefanyk, together with the leaders of the new government, fled to Kiev where, on January 22, 1919, the Union of the Western (Austrian) and Eastern (Russian) Ukraine was promulgated.

When he returned to Russiv, Stefanyk found that, with the assistance of the Entente, the Polish armies had occupied Lviv and the entire Western Ukrainian territory. As painful as it was, he had no other choice but to reconcile himself to the new police state. As a political man of importance, he still enjoyed some influence and served his people by preventing the Poles from committing revengeful atrocities against the Ukrainians who would not submit to them. Particularly was he vocal during the Polish so-called "pacification", in which Polish armed bands, at the orders of the Warsaw government, cruelly maltreated the Ukrainian population in his country. By offering himself to the police authorities as a scapegoat to be beaten to death he saved the entire village of Russiv from the calamities that had befallen the Ukrainian population elsewhere under the Polish power.

Shortly after the war, his father and both his brothers died, and he, together with his three young sons, was left desolate on the property that still belonged to him. His material circumstances began to deteriorate sharply. No royalties for his work were forthcoming, the remuneration for his service as a member of the Austrian Parliament ceased completely, his land yielded little, and no Maecenas appeared to assist him financially. As a result, he found himself at the limit of his resources, and was forced to seek any means of subsistence regardless of its source. He did not have to wait long for temporary relief from his straitened circumstances.

Stefanyk's cultural relations with the Ukrainian SSR began in 1924. The Communist regime began to consider him the greatest socialist writer of the land, and many editions of his works were published in Kiev and Kharkiv, for which he received substantial honorariums. In addition, the Commissariat of Education of Ukraine offered him a life-time pension, and he was invited by the All-Ukrainian Academy of Sciences to accept the honour of becoming an Academician. Upon the advice of his close friends, he accepted the pension, on the basis that the money belonged to the Ukrainian people, but refused the membership in the Academy, apparently feeling that this body was dominated by its counterpart in Moscow. He was twice invited to visit Kiev, but declined the proposals; the second time his reason was that the Communist government under Stalin was forcibly collectivizing the peasants' lands, imposing an artificial famine on the population, and liquidating the Ukrainian political, social and literary leaders who were opposed to such inhuman measures. On that account he also rejected the pension which he had been receiving from the Russian-dominated Ukrainian government. Of Communists, it is said, he was "panically" afraid. However, he stressed the fact that he would always remain "a supporter of the Great Ukraine," as the Eastern part of his country was then called. His relations with the Soviet Ukraine nevertheless began to weaken soon after 1930. Obviously, it was because the Soviet government in Kiev became disenchanted with him for continuing to write in a nationalistic vein. His novelette "The Sons" revealed that tendency, and his dedication of the short work "The Boundary Line" to Mykola Khvylovyi, who was the leader of the anti-Russian group among the Ukrainian Communist literati, completed the severing of whatever links yet remained between Stefanyk and the Soviet Ukraine.

At about this time his health began to fail. In 1927 he felt the first symptoms of arteriosclerosis. Three years later he was partially paralyzed, but, because of the constant care of his personal physician, Dr. I. Podiuk, was eventually restored to some vigour. However, the energy that enlivened him during six decades had now left him forever. He apparently treated his condition rather lightly. To Olena Pleshkan he said: "Regardless of how ill I am, regardless that I am now a cripple, I can still reach my grave."

Stefanyk was not a practising Catholic of the Byzantine rite; but, in spite of his radical ideas, he always maintained friendly relations with the progressive clerical circles, especially with the great Metropolitan of Galicia, Andriy Sheptycky who, as a personal friend, helped him not only spiritually but materially. In 1936 he went to Lviv and, after visiting the venerable prelate, asked to be confessed by the latter's brother, Father Klymentiy. It

11

was his desire to preserve this Christian tradition of his forebears. While in Lviv, he also made arrangements with Dr. V. Simovych to have his stories, which he had written in the dialect of his district, transmuted into Ukrainian literary language. Thus far, it has not been done, and never should be, because it is precisely the dialect he used that makes his works pre-eminently poetic.

In the fall of 1936 he caught a chill which developed into pneumonia. He died on December 7. On his death bed he was surrounded by his entire family and many of his personal friends, including Ivan Didukh, who served as a model for the main character in "The Stone Cross." Absent, unfortunately, was his youngest son, who the year before had emigrated to Canada.

* * *

As indicated at the beginning of this brief study, Vasyl Stefanyk's stories are regional in character. With few exceptions, such as his poems in prose, he dealt with the people of the village of Russiv and the surrounding districts, describing the utter poverty of the destitute peasants and hirelings who existed almost at the lowest depths of human strata. Born a son of a peasant who loved the soil with all the might of his soul, he too loved it to the point of distraction, and even more those who so passionately tended it.

The fact that Stefanyk selected as his subject the poverty of the peasants who surrounded him, and depicted the episodes in which they figure in minor tones and sombre moods, does not reveal him, as many of his critics claimed, to be a pessimist and a decadent presiding over the complete impoverishment of Ukrainian villages. Actually, he is an optimist, for he presents life as he sees and feels it, making the peasants aware of their sorry predicament and thus evoking in them the longing for a better lot. It may have been vain labour, but he did believe that a brighter day would finally break for them after the many years of economic deprivation.

Nowhere in Europe was the poverty among the peasants so evident as in his particular region. He demonstrated it with such keenness that the entire scene he created seemed an immense exaggeration. It was not.

If one doubts this statement, let him consider the hundreds of thousands of people who, since the end of the nineteenth century, emigrated to Canada, the United States and Brazil. Those countless numbers should convince him that it was sheer lack of livelihood that caused them with heavy hearts to uproot themselves from their native soil and seek foreign, often hostile, lands beyond the oceans, uncertain where they were to settle and what destiny awaited them.

The pathos of such an emigration is masterfully particularized in Stefanyk's story "The Stone Cross," in which a representative family, that of Ivan Didukh (a real character), is compelled by force of economic circumstances to abandon its precious soil and, with heart-felt pain, go in search of a new habitat where life might be more endurable. With such passion did Stefanyk render the tragedy of this family that his father-in-law was forced to advise him not to write so poignantly or he would die from such an acute exertion. This was one of his longer masterpieces and one which he liked best. All that the Ukrainian peasant felt is here.

Many a time Stefanyk saw masses of Ukrainian peasants pass through the Cracow railway station in utter disarray, with mothers seeking their lost children, wives their husbands, separated families weeping as they were packed like cattle into train coaches that were to take them to western ports, swindled on the way by unscrupulous agents. His sensitive soul could not endure the sight of such sufferings, and he could not do otherwise but write in the manner he did in order to make the authorities aware of the injustices done to those unfortunates on their way out of their land which could not feed them and where families, in numerous cases, had to sell whatever property they still possessed and live crowded together in single cottages with no idea where their next meal would come from. The plight of the peasants was delineated in these stories with an ardour that boded disastrous effects for Stefanyk's mind. Hence Hamorak's distressed warning to his son-in-law to beware the strain of such an impetuous labour.

It must be understood that the Ukrainian village, for the most part, was composed of two sorts of peasants. Most of them were destitute, some altogether landless; a few were rich, and for them the former worked as servants and hirelings. Between the two groups, enmity was not rare; it often led to bloody confrontations as the wealthy villagers sought to exploit the poor to the utmost. Above these classes reigned the landlord who, in many instances, owned vast arable tracts. To him all peasantry deferred. There existed yet another class, that of the gentry who lived mostly in towns, many of them impoverished but still preserving their attitudes of superiority.

A few of Stefanyk's stories are crude in character. Presenting the life of the peasants as it actually was, he could not, as a realist, help making them express themselves in a manner that was natural to them, whether at home or in a tavern to which they often escaped to gain some relief in drunkenness, and so, at least while the intoxication lasted, forget their misery. Their intemperance was a vice, but Stefanyk's sympathy was always with them, regardless of how they behaved. In fact, the crudity, with which his stories are replete, adds to the literary value of the depiction of such types. Emile Zola by far exceeds Stefanyk's characters in vulgarity. Certain modern writers are even more loquacious in that respect.

The reaction of the peasants against their oppressors at times assumed tragic proportions, as in "The Arsonist," in which an indigent rustic sets fire to the estate of his former employer for whom he had toiled for many years and who sends him packing when the old man is no longer able to work. "The Thief" is another example where a poor landowner, about to be robbed, catches the culprit and, with the help of his neighbour, after playing with the robber as a cat would with a mouse, murders him. Both these stories are based on events that actually happened. Stefanyk, however, changed them somewhat. In reality, the rich peasant, whose possessions were destroyed, restored them and continued to thrive, and the thief was saved from a horrible death by the landowner's wife. It is somewhat baffling why Stefanyk altered these incidents.

Another factual event is fictionally related in "Big News," in which a widowed father, seeing no relief from misery for himself and his two small daughters, out of sheer despair drowns one of them, sets the older free as she pleads with him to spare her, then goes to the police to report his deed. In Stefanyk's eyes, the man is not a criminal. He loves his children, and commits the crime out of deep love for them, to save them from the tribulations he knows lie in store for them. Salt being an expensive commodity for a peasant, he shows his love for the girls by salting the boiled potatoes which is the last meal they receive from him. To the daughter who is saved he gives a cane with which to protect herself from vicious dogs before she reaches the village. These small acts of compassion reveal that the author is certainly on the side of the murderer. Some time later Stefanyk had an occasion to speak with the older daughter who told him exactly what happened.

The father in "Maple Leaves" likewise appears cruel to his children when he speaks to and of them in a manner so merciless as to make even a hard-crusted man's eyes moist with tears. Yet he loves them immensely. When at dawn he goes to work on his landlord's fields, he leaves them with their dying mother, who had only recently given birth to a new child, and instructs his oldest, six-year-old, boy to place a lighted candle in her hands when she is about to expire. So great is his love for them that, even at such a crucial moment, he goes to toil so that they may have enough to eat. Every peasant in Stefanyk's stories loves his offspring, in spite of the severity with which he addresses them. The seeming pitilessness is only a means whereby the father relieves his worry about his children's miserable future.

The seemingly inhuman manner with which grown children, especially those who are married, treat their old parents is no less pathetic. In "Children," the hoary father's complaints about the wrongs he and his wife suffer at the hands of their son and daughter-in-law may be justifiable; but if one considers that they are both unable to work and that there is not enough food to go around, the matter assumes a different aspect. To the younger ones, who have to work hard, the parents are only an insufferable burden. If their conduct towards the old is mean, who is actually to blame?

With such acrimony does Stefanyk deal with the penury of the peasants that at times it appears as if he himself were struggling with some herculean, malicious Fate which has no mercy on the human beings it takes pleasure in trampling into the soil which they love with all the fibres of their hearts, and causing that very soil to draw out of them the last ounce of their strength with all the pain that it can inflict. In that grim mood, the author even allows certain of his characters to speak brutally to the Creator for making their lives a continuous series of ordeals. It is not sacrilegiously that their curses rise towards Him; rather they are stern entreaties with which the wretched creatures plead with Him to deliver them from the pains and griefs to which they are subjected. "The Sons," "The Sin," "The Boundary Line" are among the tales in which Stefanyk goes to the extremities of that kind.

In spite of the tragic tenor of all his works, it cannot be said that Stefanyk is devoid of a certain amount of humour. Many of the phrases used by his characters in relating their misfortunes make one smile, but it is with tearful drollery that he manipulates their monologues and dialogues, all of which are rendered amid the dire conditions in which they are forced to live. "The Pious

Woman" and "The Schoolboy" are among those with such tragi-comical features. The greatest of them is perhaps "The Signature" in which a young schoolgirl teaches some old landowners to write their names so that they can scribble their signatures on legal documents instead of marking them with a cross; for continuing to sign them in such an illiterate manner means paying a notary and witnesses who charge heavily for this petty service. So eager are the old men to learn at least that precious little that, straining all their energy, they make the table creak as they press their chests against it with galling exertion.

The main feature of Stefanyk's style is its laconism, a style of narration which, at times, is more difficult to maintain than the more expansive composition of a lengthy novel. Each word, each phrase of his seems to equal an ample sentence, and a few paragraphs – an extensive tale. In most cases, it is not a story that is rendered but a concentrated episode from the life of a person. This procedure effects an enormous economy in the depiction of settings and characters, all of which are implied in the manner in which the author composes his monologues and dialogues. It is often apparent that, having selected his character, the creator stands aside and lets him evolve his particular experience with utmost brevity, as the spirit moves him, in a realistic or psychological manner. In so doing, it often results that a given episode assumes the feature of a filigree, or a tiny jewel emerging from the highly skilled hand of an artist. Laconism, let us repeat, is the essence of Stefanyk's works. His sentences are short, at times jumbled, but were one word of them omitted or some other added, the exact sense of the meaning would be lost.

With whatever he wrote, Stefanyk was seldom satisfied. He continued to polish his works and change them to the point where one version was almost completely different from another. It was rarely that he corrected his sentences on the pages on which they were written. Having put them on paper, he reread them, and if the matter was not to his satisfaction, he would tear up the sheet and begin anew. When he had finally completed his work tolerably well, the floor around him was strewn with heaps of discarded stationery. The apparent simplicity of his stories is deceptive. He required much time to produce a work that brought him relative peace of mind. He was particularly concerned with the conclusions of his stories, for it was there that the climax of his episodic narrations often lay.

Pehaps no other author we know was so imbued with the love

for the soil as was Stefanyk. To such a degree did he revere it that, at times, he became its lyricist, personifying it to the extent of making it speak to the husbandman toiling upon it, entreating him to gather the bread it yielded. A fine example of this fancy is to be found in "The Arsonist."

Most of his fiction and études are suffused with impressionistic lyricism. The work best illustrating that quality is "My Word" in which almost every sentence imparts some important, but painful, experience in his life. It is actually a poem in prose, as are to a lesser degree most of the other diminutive presentations of the people into whose souls he delved not as an ethnographer but as an artist whose chief aim was to comprehend their spiritual excellence. Toma Kobzey understood him well when he called Stefanyk "the great sculptor of the Ukrainian peasants' souls." As such, the artist could not help but be lyrical.

With such concentration did he seek to convey the psychic essence of his characters that, by his own admission, every detail about them that he put on paper made him fearful of losing his mind. It was, therefore, with great reluctance that he would begin the description of his dismal types, whom he presented in all their naked reality, without any sentimentalism to dissipate the gloom besetting them. If an obstinate critic still insists that Stefanyk went beyond the bounds of pessimism, he must be made aware that it was the pessimism related to a downtrodden man who, when struck again and again by the flail of his fate, could not but cry in pain to high heaven.

From his lyrical impressionism Stefanyk occasionally lapsed into expressionism, as he did in "Grandpa Hritz" where the oppressed peasants finally begin to feel the strength, which their educated children inspired them with, and react against those who, for long centuries, had been treating them and their ancestors with grievous injustice. It is with the sure spirit of optimism that he makes old Hritz say enthusiastically: "A single potent word made the earth in towns rumble under our feet, and more than one corner timber in a rich man's house was loosened." This expressionistic assertion implies the fear which the well-to-do felt in their cosy homes, manors and palaces when the poor folk raised their voices in protest against the harm that had been inflicted on them and their forebears of distant generations.

Many such examples of expressionism verging on hyperbole are to be found in Stefanyk's works. It is for that reason that he is so difficult to translate into other languages. As a result much of the poetry inherent in his stories is lost to those who are not able to read him in the original. The translator, the poor devil who does his best, finds himself mortified in striving to retain Stefanyk's exact idiom in another tongue.

Stefanyk's post-bellum works number twenty-three items. Eight of them were included in the collection entitled *The Earth* (his fifth), which was published in Lviv in 1926. The rest were printed in various newspapers and journals until they were finally incorporated in several editions of his complete works shortly after 1933 when he ceased to produce altogether.

The second period of his creativity actually began in 1916, when, in Vienna, his friends forced him to resume writing. As mentioned previously, the first literary piece he gave them was "The Children's Adventure," which was later included in *The Earth*. The first work of this collection was "Mother Earth" and was dedicated to his father whom, in his later years, he began to admire as an exemplary peasant with a fervent love for the soil. Another memorable story was "Maria," in which he portrayed a strong-minded patriotic woman who gave three of her sons to fight for the liberty of Ukraine. In it he brilliantly described the Ukrainian Sitch Sharpshooters whose struggle in defence of their country's freedom, against terrible odds, is one of the most heroic episodes in Ukraine's history. In "The Baby-Watchers" and "The Sin" he wrote sympathetically of those mothers who had borne illegitimate children during the war.

Of supreme significance in that collection is "The Sons," in which Stefanyk recounts the sorry existence of an old man who lost his only two sons in the War of Liberation. As the hoary tiller painfully harrows his land, he speaks to God, as one would to a neighbour, and in the most poetic eloquence upbraids Him for the woeful infliction He let befall him. Upon his return to his humble cottage, he kneels before the icons and in a fervent prayer entreats the Mother of God to be his housewife now that he is alone. His imagination becomes vocal as he sees her and her Son in the middle and his two sons on either side of them. With an ardour such as only the aggrieved soul of a peasant can evoke, he tells her with resignation: "You gave one son, I gave two." In world literature one would have to search far and wide to find a masterpiece as powerful as "The Sons."

The stories of Stefanyk's second period are more mature than those of the first. In them he still clings to peasant themes, but his words are harsher, his phrases more stringent, as if he were seeking to cast out all the pain, sorrow and grief that had accumulated in him during his entire life. In Ukrainian as well as in world literature, Vasyl Stefanyk is a phenomenon who, fired "by the slings and arrows of outrageous fortune," created a work which is a mighty outcry of trenchant protest against nature's malevolence and man's inhumanity to man.

C. H. Andrusyshen,
Department of Slavic Studies,
University of Saskatchewan.

The Stone Cross

For as long as the villagers could remember Ivan Didukh as a landholder, he had always owned only one horse and a small wagon with an oak shaft. He would hitch the horse on the nearside and himself on the off-side. For the horse Ivan had a breastband and neck-strap of leather, and on himself he would put a small breast-band made of rope. He did not need a neck-strap because he could come to a stop with his left hand, perhaps better.

When they were hauling sheaves from the field, or manure to the field, the veins stood out on both the horse and Ivan, their traces strained and were just as taut as instrument strings whether drawing uphill or dragging on the ground on the downward roll. The horse crept up the hill slowly, as though he were on ice, and the vein of Ivan's forehead swelled large, as if he had been struck across the brow with a stick. From above, the horse looked as though Ivan had hung him up on the end of the shaft by the neck-strap for some great offence, while Ivan's left hand appeared entwined with a net of blue veins as with a blue steel chain.

Often in the morning, before sunrise, Ivan would make his way to his land up the field path. He would walk without his breast-band on the right hand side of the road, the shaft seemingly under his arm. The horse and Ivan stepped along briskly, because both had had a good night's rest. Whenever they happened to go downhill, they ran, leaving behind them wagon tracks, hoof-marks and Ivan's very broad footprints. The herbs and stalks along the path swayed in all directions after the wagon passed, shedding the dew on those tracks. But sometimes during their fastest trot, right in the middle of the hill Ivan would start limping and bring the horse to a halt. He would sit down beside the road, pick up his bare foot with his hand and wet it with saliva to find the spot where the thistle had embedded itself.

"Bah! It would be better to scrape this foot with a hoe rather than wash it with spit," grumbled Ivan angrily.

"Grandpa Ivan, use the whip on that plow-horse,[1] and make him run if he eats oats."

Seeing Ivan's predicament, someone from the neighbouring field was poking fun at him. But Ivan had long since grown accustomed to such jokers and quietly continued removing the

---

1 Meaning Ivan himself.

thistle. If he failed to draw it out, he would drive it in deeper with his fist and, rising to his feet, say:

"Never mind, rot and fall out by yourself. I haven't the time to waste on you."

The villagers also called Ivan "perelomaniy."[2] He had a defect in his waist and always walked stooped, as if weighted down by two iron hooks pulling the trunk of his body toward his feet. It was said that he was windswept[3].

When he had returned home from the army he found neither his father nor his mother alive, only a small dilapidated hut. And all the wealth his father had left him was a chunk of a hill-top, the steepest and poorest land in the whole village. Women had been digging for sand on that hill, and now it yawned with ravines and caves under the heavens, like some terrible giant. No one had ever plowed or sown it, and it was not surveyed or marked in any way. Ivan was the only one who took to digging and sowing his share of the land. Both he and his horse would haul the manure up to the hill, and then Ivan would carry it, a sackful at a time, to the top. Occasionally, his loud voice would drop down on the cultivated fields below:

"Confound it! I'll dash you down so hard that every thread'll fly apart, you're so heavy!"

But apparently he never did fling any sack too hard, because he hated to lose it, and just slid it down gently from his shoulders to the ground.

One evening he told his wife and children about the following experience:

"The sun was scorching hot, not only scorching but scattering fire. And I was down on my knees, inching upwards with a sack of manure so hard that the skin on my knees seemed to be ripping off. Sweat was seeping out of every hair of mine, and my mouth felt so salty it was bitter. I hardly made it to the top. And on the top such a light breeze blew on me, such a light, very light one! And then, for all you know, within a minute my spine felt as if it was being stabbed with knives. I thought I was done for!"

Ever since this misfortune Ivan always walked bent at the waist, and people nicknamed him "perelomaniy."

But though that hill broke his body, it yielded him good crops. Ivan drove in piles and posts, carried up hard lumps of sod to

2 Fractured one.

3 A belief that one suffered some such calamity because an evil wind had blown on him.

place around them, and thus surrounded his part of the property to prevent the fall and spring rains from washing away the manure and carrying it into gullies. He spent his whole life on that hill.

The older he got, the harder it became for him, broken as he was, to come down from the hill.

"Such a doggone hill that it plunges you headlong!"

Often, when the setting sun found him on top of the hill, it cast his and the hill's shadows far across the cultivated fields. Ivan's shadow, spread across those fields, looked like some giant bent at the waist. He would then point his finger at his shadow and say to the hill:

"Look, you poor devil, just look how you've bent me into a bow! But as long as my feet carry me, you must produce bread! You'll not eat the sun and drink the rains for doing nothing!"

Ivan's sons and wife worked in the other fields which he bought with the money he brought home from the army. His own greatest concern was the hill.

In the village Ivan was also known for his going to church only once a year, at Easter, and for disciplining his chickens. He trained them so well that none dared set foot in the yard and scratch in the manure. If any of them made the slightest scratch with its tiny claw, a spade or a stick put an end to it. Even if his wife had prostrated herself before him crosswise, it would have been in vain.

There was one other thing: Ivan never ate at the table, but always on the bench.

"I've been a hired servant, and later I served ten years in the army, but I was never near a table. The food doesn't go down to my stomach well at the table."

Such was Ivan, odd in nature and in work.

II

Ivan's house was full of guests, all landholders and their wives. He had sold everything he owned because his sons, together with his wife, were determined to go to Canada, and the old man, finally, had to give in.

Ivan invited the whole village.

Standing before his guests, with a glass of whiskey in his right hand, he was apparently petrified, because for a long while he could not utter a single word. When in the end his speech was restored, he began to stammer:

23

"I thank you kindly, all of you fellow-landholders and your wives, for the respect you've given me and my wife and for treating us as you would one of yourselves. . . ."

He did not continue with what was yet to be said, nor did he drink to anybody, but merely stood there with a dull look in his eyes, nodding his head, as if he were saying a prayer and stressing every word of it with each nod.

When, at times, some powerful undercurrent rolls a large stone out of the water and deposits it on the shore, then that stone remains on the shore heavy and inert. The sun chips the old accumulation of silt off it and paints over its surface tiny phosphorescent stars. The stone glimmers with lifeless lustre reflected from the sunrise and the sunset, gazing with its stony eyes upon the living water and grieving that it is no longer burdened by its aqueous weight as in the ages past. From the shore it looks on the water as on some lost happiness.

As that stone stares at the water, so did Ivan gaze at his guests. He shook his grey hairs, as if they were a mane forged of steel threads, and concluded:

"I thank you all very kindly, and may God give you whatever you desire. God grant you health, my old friend Mikhaylo!"

He handed Mikhaylo a glass of liquour, and both kissed each other's hands.

"Ivan, my dear crony, may God grant you long life, and may the merciful Lord bring you to your new place and, by His grace, help you to become a landholder again!"

"May God allow it! Come, my dear friends, help yourselves. . . . I had hoped to have you around this table as guests at my son's wedding, but it turned out to be different. The times are now such that what our fathers and grandfathers never knew, that we must know. It's the Lord's will! Help yourselves, friends, and excuse me for what's lacking."

Picking up a glass of whiskey, he walked over to the women sitting at the other end of the table, near the bed.

"Timofiy's woman,[4] dear godmother of my son, I want to drink to you. Looking at you, I seem to recall our younger years. My, oh my! What an attractive, hardy lass you used to be! Many a night I spent with you dancing. And in a dance you went like a shuttle in a loom – so straight! Where are those years of ours now, my dear, where are they? Come now, eat hearty. And forgive me

[4] Colloquial for a woman bearing her husband's Christian name, Timothy.

for recalling those dances now that I'm old and hoary. Be so good as to eat. Please do."

He glanced at his old wife who was weeping among the women, and pulled out a handkerchief from inside his shirt front.

"Old wife, here's a handkerchief for you. Wipe yourself nicely. I don't want to listen to any bawling here! Look after the guests. There'll be plenty of time to cry. You'll cry so much yet that your eyes will trickle out."

He joined the men again, and was shaking his head.

"I'd say something, but I'd better keep quiet out of respect for the holy pictures in the house, and for you, too, my kind friends. But just the same, may God prevent any good man from falling into a woman's way of reasoning. Look there, see how she's crying? And why? Because of me? Is it because of me that you're crying, my housemate? Did I uproot you from your home in your old age? Be quiet, stop sobbing, or I'll pull out those grey braids of yours, and you'll go to Hamerica[5] like a Jewess."[6]

"Crony Ivan, leave your wife alone. She's not your enemy, nor is she your children's enemy. She's only sorry for her family and her village."

"Timofiy's woman, if you don't know what you're talking about, don't give me even a tinkle. She's sorry! What about me? Am I going there jumping for joy?"

He gnashed his teeth, sounding like a handmill, threatened his wife with his mallet-like fist, and began beating his chest.

"Take an axe and whack me right here, where the liver is, and maybe my gall bladder will burst, because I can't stand it any longer! People, such is my grief, such grief it is that I don't know what's happening to me."

III

"Please, friends, help yourselves without fuss and bother, and excuse us for neglecting you, because we're already travelers. And don't be surprised at old me for chiding my wife a little; but it's not for nothing, oh, it's not for nothing! This would've never happened but for her and her sons. The sons can read and write, so when they got some kind of a letter into their hands, when they got some sort of a map, and when they convinced the old woman.

5 A corruption for America.
6 Usually with hair closely cropped.

then they filed and filed away at me until they had me cut through. For two years nothing was talked about in the house but Canada and Canada. And when they had me up against the wall, and when I saw that they'd go on gnawing me in my old age if I didn't go, I went and sold everything, to the very last stick. My sons don't want to be hired hands after I'm gone, so they said to me: 'You're our father, so lead us away to some land and give us bread, because if you divide between us what you have now, we'll have little to live on.' May God help them to get that bread to eat. As for me, it doesnt' matter where I die. But, my dear friends, how am I, broken as I am, to be going on journeys? I'm worn out. My whole body is one big callus, my bones are mouldy, so much so that by the time I pull them together in the morning, I holler in pain at least ten times."

"It's all over now, Ivan. You'd better put all grief out of your head. Who knows! After you've shown us the way, we might all follow you. This country is not worth breaking your heart for. This land can't support so many people or bear so many woes. The muzhik can't do it, the land can't do it, even both of them can't do it. No locusts here, but there's no wheat either. While taxes are piling up! Where once you paid a lev,[7] now you pay five; once you ate salted pork, now you eat potatoes. Oh, they sure have got us in a squeeze; they've got us so tight in their clutches that no one can wrest us from them, unless we get out of here. But one day calamity will visit this land, and people will slaughter one another. You've got nothing to grieve for."

"Thank you for what you've said, but I don't accept it. Sure enough, people will slaughter one another. But isn't God angry at those who sell their land? Now no one wants land, only bills of exchange and dealings with banks. The young landholders have become smarter – the kind of swindlers that aren't on fire to get land. Look at that old fiddle over there, my wife. Can one let her tackle a business? She's but a hollow reed. Just move a finger and she'll get in trouble. And do you think she'll last the trip? Why, she'll tumble over into some ditch where dogs will tear her to pieces, and we'll be driven along without even getting a chance to look at her. How can God bless such children? Old woman, come here!"

Ivan's wife stepped forward. She was old and withered.

"Katerina, what are you mulling over in your head? Where will

---

[7] Monetary unit, usually a gold coin, used in that part of the country.

I lay you into a grave? Or will the fish eat you up? For a big fish you're not enough even for one bite. Just look!"

He stretched the skin on his wife's arm and showed it to the people.

"Nothing but skin and bones. Is she fit to leave the clay-stove?[8] You were a decent woman, you worked hard, you were thrifty, but in your old age you're starting on a long journey. Look there, do you see your journey and where your Canada is? There!"

And, through the window, he pointed at the graveyard.

"You weren't too keen on going to this Canada, so we'll go wandering about the world, drifting apart in our old age like leaves in the field. God only knows what will happen to us . . . so I want to ask for your forgiveness in front of these our people. Just as we took our marriage vows before them, so now, with them present, I want to ask for your forgiveness before we die. Maybe they'll throw you into the sea, so that I won't even see you go, or they may toss me overboard without you seeing it. So forgive me, my wife, for chiding you so often that, at times, I wronged you perhaps and made you suffer. Forgive me once, forgive me twice, forgive me three times."

They kissed. Ivan's wife fell into his arms, and he said:

"My poor dear, that I should be taking you to your far-away grave!"

But no one heard these last words, because from the woman's table there sprang a gust of weeping that sounded like a blast of wind from amongst sharp swords, and bowed the muzhiks' heads down to their chests.

IV

"And now, my old wife, go among the housewives and see to it that each one has enough of what's coming to her. And take a drink yourself so that for once in your life I will see you drunk.

"And of you, my friends, I have two favours to ask. It may be that some day my sons will send a letter to the village post office to say that my wife and I have both passed away. So I would ask you that you arrange to have a Mass said for the repose of our souls and that you gather at a little dinner like today and say the Lord's Prayer for us. Maybe the good Lord will charge us with fewer sins. Money for these things I'll leave with Yakiw, because

8 The top of a clay-stove in a village cottage was flat. The peasants slept there and, in winter, kept warm.

he's a young and honest fellow and will not pocket grandpa's kreutzers."

"We'll arrange it, we'll arrange it, and we'll say the Lord's Prayer for both of you. . . ."

Ivan fell into musing. Some sort of embarrassment was showing on his face.

"Don't be surprised at the old man, and don't laugh at hoary grandpa. I myself am somehow ashamed to tell you this, but it seems to me that it would be a sin not to tell you about it. You all know I placed a small cross on my hill. It was hard moving it, and hard heaving it up to the top, but I did place it there. It's so heavy that the hill can't get rid of it and must hold it on its back, just as it held me. I want to leave that much of a memorial behind me."

He cupped his hands and pressed them to his lips.

"I yearn for that hill as much as a child for a nipple. There I spent my lifetime, and became crippled on it. If only I could, I'd hide it in my bosom and take it with me wherever I go. I yearn for the tiniest thing in the village, for the smallest child, but I'll never stop yearning for that hill."

His eyes quivered with great grief, and his face trembled like black tilled land trembles under the sun.

"Last night, as I lay in the barn, I kept thinking and thinking: 'Merciful Lord, what great sin have I committed that You should drive me away far beyond the world's seas?' All my life I just worked and worked and worked. Often, as the day was ending, I'd fall on my knees in the field and fervently pray to God: 'Lord, never deny me a morsel of black bread, and I'll always toil, unless I'm unable to move either my arms or legs. . . .'

"And then I was stricken with such grief that I gnawed at my knuckles, tore out my hair, and rolled on the straw like a beast. An evil thought struck me! I don't know just how and when I found myself under a pear tree with a rope. In a moment I'd have hanged myself. But the merciful Lord knows what He is doing. I recalled my cross, and in a flash I was myself again. Oh-h, did I run, did I run up to my hill! Within an hour I was already sitting beneath that cross. There I sat for a long, long time, and somehow I felt relieved.

"Look, I'm standing here before you and talking to you, but that hill does not leave my mind. I simply see it, never stop seeing it. I'll be dying and still see it. I'll forget everything, but I won't forget it. On it I forgot the songs I knew, and on it I lost the strength I had."

A tear-drop rolled down his cheeks, like a pearl down a cliff.

"I beg you, friends, never to pass by my hill when on the Holy Sunday you'll be having the fields blessed. Let some youngster run up and sprinkle the cross with holy water, because, you know, the priest wouldn't go up that hill. I beg this of you very humbly. Never pass up my cross. I'll pray to God for you in the other world, only do carry out grandpa's request."

He spoke as if he wanted to meekly prostrate himself before them, as if with his kind, grey eyes he wanted to embed that wish forever in the hearts of his guests.

"Ivan, godfather of my son, do forget your grief and throw it far away from you. We will always remember you, now and forever. You were a decent man, never treated anyone insolently, never overplowed or oversowed anyone else's land as if it were your own, never touched a kernel that wasn't yours. Oh, no! People will remember you and will never pass up your cross on the Holy Sunday."

Thus did Mikhaylo comfort Ivan.

V

"I've already told you everything, dear friends. And now, whoever likes me, will drink with me. The sun is already behind the mound, and you haven't yet drunk a glass of whiskey with me. While I'm still in my house and have guests at my table, I'll drink to them, and anyone who's fond of me will do me that favour too."

Drinking now began in all earnest, the kind of drinking that turns muzhiks into senseless boys. Soon Ivan, already drunk, asked the musicians to be called to play for the young people who filled the whole yard.

"Hey, all of you! You've got to dance so hard that the earth will rumble, so that not a single blade of grass will remain on the threshing ground!"

In the house everybody drank, everybody talked, but nobody listened. Talk flowed for talk's sake, because something just had to be said, even if only to the wind. It was mere gibberish.

"When I groomed him, he was groomed. Whichever was black looked as if dusted with silver over black, and whichever was white, looked like butter covered lightly with snow. With me horses were always in fine fettle. The Emperor himself could have ridden them! And I had money, ah, did I have it!"

"If I could find myself in the middle of such a desert where only I and God would be there! So that I could walk about like a wild beast, not seeing those taverners or gentry or priests! Then it could be rightly said that I'm a gentleman myself! And this land, let it go and collapse, let it collapse right now for all I care. Why feel sorry? They flogged and tortured our fathers, they harnessed them in yokes, and now they don't give us a morsel of bread to gobble. . . . Oh-h, if I only had my way! . . ."

"No collector has ever been found who seized anything of ours for taxes, oh no! There was a Czech, there was a German, there was a Pole, but, excuse the language, they took shit. But when a Mazur[9] was appointed, he found a small sheepskin jacket even far out under the cherry tree. I'm telling you, a Mazur is trouble. It wouldn't be a sin even to burn his eyes out."

There was much talk about everything, but it was scattered in the most diverse directions, like rotten trees in an old forest.

Ivan's and old Mikhaylo's singing was cutting into all that hubbub, clamour, screaming, and into the plaintive merriment of the fiddles. It was the kind of singing that is often heard at weddings when old muzhiks gather enough enticement and break into oldtime songs. The tones of those ditties encountered difficulties in the old throats, as if calluses had formed not only on the hands of the singers, but also in their windpipes. The words they sang were like yellow autumn leaves driven by the wind over the frozen ground, gathering here and there, in every gully, their broken edges quivering as if they were about to die.

Thus did Ivan and Mikhaylo sing about their youth which had caught up with them on a cedar bridge, and passed away without ever wanting to return to them, not even as a guest.

Whenever they struggled to reach a high note, they squeezed each other's hands, but so hard that their joints creaked; and whenever they came upon some very plaintive passage, they leaned toward each other, their foreheads touching, and grieved. They embraced each other's neck, kissed, pounded their chests and the table with their fists, and with their rusty voices brought upon themselves such overpowering sorrow that finally they were unable to utter a single word except: "O, Ivan, my brother!" – "O, Mikhaylo, my dear friend!"

VI

"Father, do you hear? It's time to go to the train, and here you're singing as if nothing was to happen."

[9] One from the northeastern part of Poland.

Ivan stared at him stupidly, but in such a strange manner that his son paled and stepped back. Ivan laid his head in the palms of his hands and was lost in thought for a long while. Rising from the table, he walked up to his wife and took hold of her sleeve.

"Old woman, come, march – one, two, three! Come, we'll dress up like the rich and go to live like the gentry."

Both went out of the room.

As they were re-entering, everyone in the house burst into wailing. As though a cloud of lamentation hanging over the village had suddenly burst, as if human woe had broken a dam on the Danube – that was how they wept. The women wrung their hands and held them interlaced over the head of Ivan's old wife, seemingly shielding her from something that might fall from above and crush her on the spot. At the same time Mikhaylo seized Ivan by the shoulders, shaking him violently and shrieking like a madman:

"Hey, if you're a landholder, chuck those rags off, or I'll wallop you like a whore!"

But Ivan did not look that way. He grabbed his old wife by the neck and whirled into a dance with her.

"Play a polka for me the way it's played for the gentry. I'm in the money!"

The crowd was benumbed, while Ivan shook his wife in the dance impetuously as though he did not mean to let her out of his hands alive.

The sons rushed in and forcibly carried them both out of the house.

In the yard, Ivan continued to dance some sort of polka, and his wife clutched the threshold with her hands, saying as she did so:

"Did I ever wear you out, did I ever gnaw you out with these feet of mine!"

And she kept holding her hand in the air to show how much of the doorstep she had worn out.

VII

The fences along the road cracked and fell. All the people were accompanying Ivan on his way. He walked beside his old wife, hunched in his grey serge suit, dancing to an endless polka.

It was not until the whole crowd paused at the cross which

Ivan had placed on the hill that he partly regained his senses, and pointed it out to his old wife.

"See our little cross, old woman? Your name is carved on it too. Don't worry. My name is also there – mine and yours."

The Recruit's Farewell

The crimson cloud hung as if petrified in the western sky. Casting its whitish shafts around it, the twilight made it resemble the gory head of some saint. From behind that head the rays of the sun were still looming.

A large crowd of people stood around in the yard. The light from the west was reflected from them as from a red rock – hard and firm. Many people were still pouring out from the porch. They emerged sadly, as if they had just viewed one deceased.

Behind them appeared a young man with his head closely cropped. All eyes were fastened on him. It seemed to those assembled that that head, which now seemed to glow in the crimson light, was destined to fall from those shoulders somewhere far away, down on the Emperor's[1] highway. In some foreign land, beneath the scorching sun, it would fall on the road and there lie abandoned.

The mother stood on the doorstep.

"You're leaving already, my dear son?"

"Yes, I am, mother."

"And who will look after us when you're gone?"

The women began to weep, the sisters wrung their hands, and the mother beat her head against the doorpost.

The father came up to his son.

"Let's get into the wagon, son, or we'll miss the train."

"Stay with me just this night, my darling boy. I tended you with so much sorrow and loving care, with so much tenderness. I

---

[1] Austrian Emperor, because Galicia was then within the Austro-Hungarian Empire.

will send you on your way with the rising sun, and will not cry. Stay another night, just one more, my child."

She took hold of her son's sleeves and led him into the house. The crowd edged toward the gate.

Before long the mother reappeared with her son. Her face was as white as chalk.

"My son," asked the father, "who will hoe the corn for me now?"

The men groaned loudly. The father leaned his head against the wagon and shook like a leaf.

"Well, let's go."

The mother was holding him back.

"Nikolay,[2] my loved one, please don't go. Before you return the doorsteps in the house will warp and its corners will rot away. You will not find me here again. Perhaps you yourself will not come back."

She clasped her son's legs.

"I'd rather lay you out on the bench and wait for your funeral."

They started to move. Whoever stood near the gate went along to accompany the recruit part of the way.

They were passing through the woods.

Leaves carpeted the road. They curved themselves into tiny copper-coloured vessels as if to journey with the recruit on the surface of autumn rains. The woods re-echoed the mother's voice, wafting it across the fields up to the distant boundary lines so that they might know that when spring bursts forth Nikolay would not be there to plow them.

They paused in the field on the other side of the woods, and there the recruit took leave of the villagers.

"Farewell, relatives and friends. If I have done you wrong in any way, be kind and forget it, and give me your blessing on my distant journey."

All removed their hats.

"Return in good health, and don't delay," they shouted.

The father and son climbed into the wagon. The mother gripped the wagon wheel.

"My precious son, take me with you. If not, I'll take a short cut across the fields and catch up with you."

"Good people, take the woman away, or she'll have her hands broken."

2 Nicholas

The men removed her by force and held her fast. The wagon moved on.

"Goodbye and good health, Nikolay!" shouted the crowd.

That night the old mother sat in the yard, wailing in a hoarse voice:

"Where am I to expect you from? Where am I to search for you?"

The daughters twittered around her, trying their best to comfort her.

Above them the canopy of the autumn sky unfolded itself. The stars twinkled like golden flowers on the smooth metallic threshing floor.

In a Tavern

Ivan[1] and Protz[2] sat beside a long table. They rolled impassioned words along the table-top and, bending forward, listened to what the table had to say. They complained, and drank. Protz's wife had been beating him, and Ivan was teaching him how to be the master of his spouse.

"Bah! May the ox be struck dead if he lets a cow beat him," said Ivan. "If my wife lifted her little finger at me, it would be the end of her. I'd pound her into a mash. Man! It's an insult and a shame to the whole world that a wife should wallop a man as if he were a horse. I'd soon bring her to her senses, so hard and fast that she wouldn't know which way to turn. I'd sharpen the axe on the grindstone and chop off her arms, right up to her elbows. Just one, two, and no more hands."

Having said that, Ivan lifted his arms aloft as if he were about to fly. He threw his head back, fixed his eyes on Protz and waited, waited to hear what Protz would say.

Protz shook his head moodily without uttering a word, for

[1] John.
[2] Colloquial for Procopius.

what was the poor fellow to say when everything he had heard was true?

"Hey! You mangy taverner, quit swaying over that book like an urchin on the limb of a tree, and give us more brandy. I pay and you serve, or else it'll be jail for me and all over with you. Don't bicker with me, just pour us some of that hooch," shouted Protz, banging the table with his fist.

The Jew laughed as he poured the brandy. The peasants began drinking. They bent toward each other and then leaned back, like two branches gently swaying in the wind.

"And do you think," Ivan said, "that I'd even wait for the gendarmes to come and take me? I'd simply cut off her hands, pull on my heavy overcoat, and go to report myself. Shame is shame, but I'd tell the authorities my wife had been beating me, and I had cut off her hands. I'd probably be kept in jail a day or two, but it might happen that I wouldn't be stuck there even an hour."

After that they drank more brandy. They drunk it with as much bitterness, making wry faces, as if they were drinking their own blood.

"Protz, my friend, here we are drinking, and you are treating me, but we're spending our own money which we earned with our bloody sweat. We're drinking our very life-blood, and helping the Jew to feed his brats. But let me, from the bottom of my heart, advise you to clamp down on your wife. Don't let her get her hands on you. Why, man! You've become the laughing-stock of the whole village! Your wife beats you and then listens whether you're still breathing, and yet you have the nerve to call yourself master in your house? I'd bridle such a woman, hitch her to a stamping-mill, take the wire whip off the peg and tame her."

Ivan took out some coins and was about to pay for the drinks, but Protz swept them down to the floor. That had made him very angry.

"Ivanko,[3] why are you ripping me, and without a knife at that? I'm in the mood to treat you because you, as someone has said, give as sound advice as one's own mother. Don't go shoving your money in front of my nose, but drink."

Again they drank.

"Or else, try to reason with her kindly. When you get home, say to your wife: 'Listen, wife, where did you make your vows to me? Was it in a church or on a rubbish heap? Were we married by

[3] Diminutive of Ivan.

a priest or by a rabbi? If you lay those hands of yours on me, I'll cut them off. Go, bring in the stool and the axe, and we'll settle our accounts.' Just lay the law down to her, and maybe you'll frighten her."

"Ivanko, my dear chap, you don't know my wife. Her heart is so hard she couldn't be frightened by a hangman. Whenever I try to threaten her, she rips me with anything she has in her hands. May the doctors rip her like that after her death! 'You squanderer,' she shouts, 'you drag everything you see to the tavern, and yet you think you're going to treat me rough?' I'm telling you, my friend, she has beaten me so, flayed me so, that I'll simply have to leave home. But I keep saying to myself: 'Maybe God will wither her hands without my help, maybe God will at last grant me that wish.' "

"Wait for God, wait, you fool, and in the meantime she'll beat you so hard you'll be flapping in the wind. So, that's the kind of a boss you are to your wife – like a willow peg in a yoke. It would be a waste even to spit on such a man."

Protz coughed till he was blue in the face. Ivan put his knuckles to his mouth and gnawed them. Then he ground his teeth so fiercely that the sound could be heard all over the tavern.

"You there, taverner! You have a learned head, Jew. That's why you're able to skin us the way you do. Tell me, is there a rule that lets a woman thrash a man? Is there such a law? You've been reading books till you've become bleary; you must have come across it somewhere. Because if the Emperor[4] has written such a law, then I want to know about it. If he has given such permission, then let my wife beat me too. I'll fold my hands across my chest and let her club away. If it's the Emperor's law, then let the Emperor have his way."

The Jew said that in all his reading he had never come across such a law. He then told Protz it was time he went home, or his wife would be scolding him.

Protz spat, opened his eyes wide, and looked at the Jew for a long time. He wanted to abuse him but thought better of it, and got up from the bench.

On the way home he shouted at the top of his voice, for all the village to hear:

"Yes, but she's not scared of me the least bit . . . not the least bit. . . .

"But I'll cut off her hands, prune her like a willow. How could

4 Austrian Emperor.

36

she do such a thing? When we were first married, a stork used to nest on the roof of the house, but now? He's gone! Where, where's the end to it all?"

He could be heard intoning to himself: "Where, where, oh where is the end to it all?"

As he neared home his voice gradually subsided, and at the gate he became silent altogether.

Mother's Little Son

Early on a Saturday morning Mikhaylo's[1] wife ran outdoors and in a resonant voice said to herself:

"Well, I wonder where the little scamp has disappeared. He must be somewhere in the yard, scratching and puttering around like a chicken. Just try and keep him in the house! I want to comb his hair, but he's nowhere to be found."

In a moment she went into the barn to see whether he was with Mikhaylo.

"Of all things! Haven't you any more sense than to keep the boy with you in the cold instead of sending him indoors? Come into the house, Andriyko,[2] and I'll give you an apple, such a nice red one!"

"Don't go, you silly boy, mother is fibbing. She wants to comb your hair and is coaxing you into the house," said Mikhaylo, breaking into laughter.

"By God, this man has outlived his sanity! Why, the child could freeze here beside you. Don't listen to daddy, Andriyko, he's a nitwit. Come into the house. I'll comb your hair and give you an apple and a bun. Really I will."

"Maybe you won't."

"Come, come, honest I will."

She took him by the hand and led him into the house.

[1] Colloquial for Michael.
[2] Diminutive of Andriy, Andrew.

"I'll give you a nice wash, comb your hair, and tomorrow you'll go to church with me. Mama will give you such a nice shirt and a little sash. Everybody will look at you and say: 'Look at Andriyko, isn't he pretty?' "

"And will you give me an apple, Ma?"

"Yes, yes, many."

"And a bun?"

"And a bun."

"And will you take me to church?"

"I will, I will."

"Then go ahead and comb my hair."

His mother began to wash his head. Drops of water trickled past his shirt collar and Andriyko could hardly keep from crying.

"Stand still, be quiet, and mother will wash you so nice and clean! Your face will be as white as paper, and your hair as soft as flax. You'll be the loveliest boy of them all."

"Oh, it bites!"

"Mother will comb you out, and then nothing will bite. You will feel so light, you'll see!"

"And when you comb my hair and give me an apple and a bun, will you let me go outside?"

"Of course. I'll dress you up and let you go far, as far as you like."

"Good, I'll go and play with Auntie's Ivan."

Mother finished washing little Andriyko, took him on her knees and was combing his hair.

"Ma, the cat that's with daddy catches such big mice, and she chokes them."

"That's because the mice eat grain and cause damage."

"What damage?"

"So that there wouldn't be anything to thresh and grind into flour."

"And what do they eat?"

"Grain, of course."

"How's that?"

"Now stop! There's no end to your questions. Tonight daddy will have to give you a haircut. Just look how long and shaggy your hair is."

"Young men's style, Ma?"

"How else? You're a young man now. There, it's all done, and yet you never want to have your hair combed. Now then, take a look in the mirror. Aren't you nice?"

Little Andriyko looked clean, as if he had been bathed. Tiny wisps of blond hair covered his neck and forehead. He had blue eyes and red lips.

His mother gave him an apple and a bun, and he hid them inside his shirt.

"I want to go to Auntie's."

"First eat your apple and then go, or the boys will take it away from you."

"I won't let them see it. I want to go to Auntie's."

"Then go, I don't mind."

She clad him in his little boots, dressed him in her small fur jacket and his father's hat and let him go outside.

"See that you don't fall down, or I'll spank you."

She sat down to sew.

"Never fear, he's as wise as an adult. As if he didn't have anyone to take after! He's the very image of Mikhaylo. And he always asks to be paid for having his hair combed."

The mother smiled and continued sewing.

"I hope he grows up to be healthy and well-behaved. He's only three and already he knows the Lord's Prayer by heart. Such a little philosopher, but also such a scamp that he turns the whole house upside down. Sometimes he gets on my nerves so much he has to be spanked. If he wasn't spanked, he'd never amount to anything."

She raised her head and looked out of the window.

"It's past noon and Mikhaylo hasn't come for his dinner yet. And the little beggar isn't back either. No doubt he's out there in the snow, and will be coughing."

*　*　*

In the evening Mikhaylo sat on the bench and held Andriyko on his knees. The fire blazed in the clay-stove,[3] lighting up the house with a glow. Mikhaylo's wife sat in front of the oven, preparing supper.

"You must have slipped into your second childhood, old man. Leave the child in peace, and quit tossing him up in the air like a pumpkin. Come to mother, Andriyko."

"But I don't want to."

"Whose boy are you – father's or mother's?" asked Mikhaylo.

"Father's."

3 See page 27.

"And who will you spank?"

"Mother."

"You little rascal! I give you apples and buns, and you're going to spank me?"

"Daddy is going to buy you a lot of apples, because you're daddy's boy."

"Say! If you waited for daddy to buy things for you, you'd never have anything."

"Now then, show us how you're going to ride a horse in the army."

The boy sat astride a poker and pranced about the room.

"That's enough, enough, Andriyko. Here's a straw. Come and skim the froth off the milk."

Andriyko rushed to the clay-stove and gathered the froth off the milk.

"Listen, Andriyko, what are you going to buy for mother?"

"Nice red boots."

"And for father?"

"I don't want to buy him anything."

"You're mother's nice boy!"

Mikhaylo took him on his knees again.

"What's your name?"

"Andriy Kossinka."

"And who are you?"

"A Ukrainian Radical."[4]

"Good. And where are you going to go?"

"To Canada."

"How will you travel there?"

"On a ship as big as a house, and across such a wide ocean, so wide, so very wide. . . ."

"Are you going to take daddy with you?"

"I'll take daddy and mamma and Auntie's Ivan, and away we'll all go."

"For pity's sake! Stop drilling the boy and pestering him with questions, or he'll fall asleep without having supper."

"But just think how smart the kid is! He knows most everything."

[4] A political party in Western Ukraine which protected the peasants' rights.

The Master Builder

At times, when the master builder drank just the right amount, not too little and not too much, he would relate one particular incident in his life. All who were in the tavern listened to him attentively, even the Jew.

"Now, my chums, I'm not going to prattle about just anything at all. I have been a master builder; I have been a man of means. The whole village will witness to that. Now I'm a scamp. Let the village witness to that too. I won't say the slightest word to deny it. I won't, because it's no sin to say what is true. But how did it happen to me? Just ask me that, if you will.

"I would come to one well-to-do, look over the place and materials, make a deal, seal it with a drink, and then – to work! I would spit into my palms, take hold of an axe, and behold – a building like a jewel would rise in the yard. From whatever side you approached it, it was a jewel.

"On Sundays I'd come out of the church and, on the way home, speculate that if I were to live just about ten years more, I would completely rebuild the village, and rebuild it in such a way that one would not be sorry if he happened to enter it. . . .

"I'd have dinner at home and go out to view the rye. On a well-trod hill I'd turn around, glance at the village, and, my dear fellows, all my buildings together would appear as light as a bird which barely touches the ground. And as I stood there and glimpsed at it all, I was as happy as a mother looking at her children. So light did I feel that I could have flown a hundred miles. . . .

"And God favored me. I would get whatever I set my mind on. And so I bought myself one small piece of cultivated land, soon another, then a cow and a few sheep. Luck was with me, things came easily into my hands, emerging lightly as if out of the water.

"And my mother, on many an occasion, would be overjoyed with me and say: 'Ah, my son, God has put a fine talent into your hands. There isn't a day or an hour that I do not thank the blessed Lord for you.' She would call: 'Old man, old man, come out of your grave, look at Ivan and see what a master he is!' And my wife, as she listened to all that, busied herself about the house as lively as a fiddle bow."

At that point Ivan would straighten up, his face beaming

with great happiness. Those who were listening looked at him somewhat sadly, but remained silent. Ivan had captivated them with his speech. He was turning the tavern into a church.

"But after that, my friends, everything went head-over-heels. It was as though one had put a feather on the palm of his hand and blown on it. That's how everything went. Not a thing was left to wind around one's little finger.

"One Sunday a man came from Luhoviska and said: 'This is my message: – our priest is inviting you to his place.' I got dressed and started out. The distance was not great, so I soon arrived at Luhoviska and went to see the priest.

"But on the way there my soul was in a dither.

"I came, kissed the priest's hand, and he told me what it was all about. He said: 'There is a need for a new church to be built in our village. We could not come to terms with that Hutzul[1] who constructs churches, so, hearing that you are a good builder, we met together and agreed that you should build the church for us.'

"Mark you, when I heard this, I broke into a sweat, as sometimes happens to a sick animal. Do you know? Even now I don't remember what I said about it to the priest, or how I left his house. Something must have dazed me.

"As I was returning home, everything in front of my eyes appeared now yellow, now black, and the wind was almost sweeping me off my feet. My head felt as if gypsy blacksmiths were pounding with hammers inside it. But all the same, thoughts came rushing one after another, and I began to wonder: 'Say! This is not to be a barn. Why, man, thousands of people place this thing into your hands, and they will all come to see that church from all the villages around.' May God protect one from such a shock as I got! I felt as if someone had bashed my head with an axe.

"I came home, but neither my wife nor my children were pleasing to my sight. I didn't say anything to any of them. All I did was stew over it.

"I lay down to sleep. I slept like a stone, sound and long, and yet I was not refreshed. I dreamed I was lying down somewhere in a cherry orchard and playing a flute. The cherry trees were in full bloom and appeared as if milk were dripping from their branches, while I was just lying there and playing the flute. Then, some-

---

[1] A man from Hutzulia, a region in Western Ukraine, in the Carpathian Mountains.

where near that orchard, a church arose, and it seemed to me that it was I who had already built it somewhere else, and it now appeared near the orchard. Suddenly there was a loud crash, as if a mountain had just collapsed. But it was that church which had exploded into dust. The bell which had stood at the very top seemed to ring so loud, but oh, so mournfully! It rang of itself. Apparently, I tried to raise myself, but the church had completely pinned me down. It seemed as though a great stream of water appeared, and ravens, so many of them, floated on it so that the water became jet-black. But the bell at the top went on ringing. The church was not there, and yet the bell at the top never stopped ringing. . . .

"I must have shouted for help, for they woke me up and brought me somewhat to my senses.

"Since then I don't remember anything. Enough to say that I spent three months in bed, and after that I didn't amount to anything. . . .

"The Hutzul did build the church in Luhoviska, and ruined me, ruined me forever. . . !"

The builder did not continue with his story, because everyone knew what happened after that.

Besides, he was unable to continue, because, having come to this point in his narrative, he would place a bottle of whiskey in front of him and drink immoderately. For that reason, those who had been sitting quietly, listening to him, started talking and expressing their pity for the builder.

"So you see, a man makes plans for this or that, but it all depends on God's power. God does not consider that this one is handsome, that one old, and still another poor. All are alike in God's sight. Whatever God intends to give, He gives to the very poorest and the very richest."

"Well, it's certainly true that no one can hide from God's power, but there are people around who can ruin a man. And this is an example: the Hutzul cast some sort of evil spell on him. Either he strewed his path with a kind of blight, or bound his reason. And look what's become of the man! He's nothing now. He's muck, that's what he is. That's just it—a man can spoil another and make him completely useless."

"You see, that's a Hutzul's nature, may he be struck dead! Look, there's that mangy taverner who simply relies on our toil, but he is better than a Hutzul. He takes your money, robs you of your possessions, but your reason he won't take away. While a Hutzul casts a spell so that a man forgets where in the world he's at. Chase a Hutzul away from your house, as you would a dog!"

"You're right! Ah, by God, you're right! Because after that Ivan went mad. He drove his wife into the grave, forced his children to leave home, and squandered whatever there was. He has a little hut, but such a horrible and shabby one that it's frightening to enter it. You wait, it won't be long before he'll leave here and go home. There he'll smash the windows, and then lie down on top of the clay-stove[2] and start singing. Now, do you think he's in his right mind? A sane man wouldn't be smashing window panes in his own house and buying new ones twice a month. It only appears that he talks sensibly, but just the same, there's something missing in his head."

"It was that infidel that made him go to pot. He entangled him so much that no one will disentangle him to the day of his death. He has broken his will-power. No work interests him anymore. Nothing. And what little he earns is all spent in the tavern."

"May the Lord God protect every good man from a fate like that. . . ."

The Pious Woman

Semen[1] and his wife returned from the church and were having their lunch. They were eating cornmeal which, again and again, they dipped into sour cream. The husband ate so voraciously that his eyes bulged out, while the wife chewed as one should, properly. From time to time she wiped her face with her sleeve because her husband would shower her with tiny specks of his spittle. Such was his manner – to smack his lips and let his saliva fly into another's eyes as hard as sand.

2 See page 27.
1 Simon or Simeon.

"Can't you close that big trap of yours a bit? It's impossible to eat a meal with one like you."

Semen continued to eat and did not close his big trap the least bit. He felt a little hurt at the way his wife had spoken, but he went on ladling the sour cream from the bowl into his mouth as before.

"He's smacking his food like four pigs. Dear me! You have as slovenly a snout as an old nag."

Semen still did not say anything. For one thing, he was somewhat to blame; but then, he wanted to fill himself up. Finally he arose, crossed himself, went outside, watered the pigs, and returned to lie down and rest.

"Look at him! He's already stuffed himself and now lies there like a log. Does he ever show his nose anywhere? No, he rots like that every Sunday, every holy day."

"Are you looking for trouble? If you are, I'll give you such a blow you won't know where you are."

"The way I feel, I could sink my teeth into you every Sunday."

"Only if a pig had horns. . . ."

"There he stands in the church like a half-slaughtered ram. The other men behave decently, while he is as bedraggled as if he was a bugbear. My face peels from shame at having such a man."

"Ah, poor me! I am in danger of losing the heavenly kingdom! Here, I work so hard all week long, and yet in church you expect me to stand at attention. You stand that way for me while I'll listen to the word of God just as I am."

"Oh, you do listen to the word of God alright! Not a thing do you remember of what the priest says in the sermon. You stand in the middle of the church like a sleep-walker. Look at you once, and your eyes have sunk into your skull; look at you again, and your mouth is wide open, like a gate; still once more, and the spittle is trickling from your mouth. When I look at you, I feel so embarrassed as if the ground under me were all aflame."

"Get away from me, you pious one. Let me get a few winks of sleep. You can chatter on and on, but I can hardly feel I have a body."

"Then don't stand in the church like a post. As soon as the priest starts reading from the book, your eyes bulge out like two onions. And you nod your head like a nag out in the sun. Trickles of spittle flow from your mouth, as thin as a spider's web. All that is needed is for you to start sputtering it all over the church. My mother used to tell me that an evil spirit steals into a man's body and makes him drowsy so that he could not hear the word of God. And there is no God in you, there really isn't."

"What on earth are you talking about? Let the devil clutch your head, not mine. What a pious one you are! For heaven's sakes! You've joined some kind of an arch-Roman society and think you're a saint already? Why, I'll beat you black and blue, and your hide will look like those lines in the book. . . Imagine, such women in a society like that! No one has ever heard or seen anything like it. One of them had a child before she married, another long after she was widowed, and the third found herself one without her husband. What a group of decent housewives! If those monks knew about it all, what sort of fine women you are, they'd drive you out of the church with cudgels. You're certainly pious ones! All you need is tails at your backs. They read books, buy holy pictures, and think they'll go to heaven alive!"

At that Semen's wife shuddered and burst out weeping.

"Then you shouldn't have married me when I already had a child. What luck I've fallen into! Why, even a bitch wouldn't have married you, such a grimy ox! You ought to thank God that I did couple myself with you, otherwise you would have been roaming about aimlessly till the day they put you into your coffin."

"I was a fool. I was greedy for a piece of your land, and so brought a witch into my house. Now I'd give even the land that's mine if I could only get rid of you."

"Oh, you won't get rid of me. I know you'd like to marry another who has land, but don't you worry, you won't beat or eat the life out of me. I'll just keep on living and you'll have to stand the sight of me, that's all there's to it."

"Then live, live till the end of the world."

"Besides, I'll still go to the society's meetings, so what can you do to me?"

"Oh no, to that society you'll never go, unless I die first. I'll throw those books out and tie you up. You won't bring me any more of that wisdom from the monks."

"Oh yes, I will, and that's that."

"Get away from me, or I'll use some ugly thing on you that will make you double up."

"Mother, dear mother, why did you make me marry such a Calvin[2] to be miserable with him all my life? Look, even on Sunday he's getting ready to beat me."

[2] It was extremely abusive among Ukrainian Greek Catholic peasants to call someone a Calvin.

"Now, hold on! Who started this quarrel anyway? And you, being so pious too! Just you wait. If that's how you act, I'll put you in your place. I'll shut your mouth a bit for you. Why, just because of this pious woman, I should leave the house? It's too bad, but I'll have to beat you up."

Semen's wife was trying to escape outside, but her husband caught her in the porch and beat her. He had to.

C. H. A.

Loss

The cow of Roman's widow fell sick. She lay on the straw and looked sadly about with her large grey eyes. Her nostrils trembled and her furry skin was quivering. She shuddered all over from a high fever. The animal smelled of disease and of the terrible but mute pain. In such cases it is a great pity that a poor beast cannot speak out and complain.

"I can plainly see that it will soon be over with her. Maybe there'd be some help if it was in her blood, but I'm sure somebody has cast an evil eye on her – I hope they trickle out of the wretch! – and now there's no help. Put your trust in God, maybe He'll comfort you."

So spoke Ilash[1] who knew all about cattle.

"O, Ilashko,[2] it is plain to see that she'll go, but if she does, I'm useless and can go too. All my life I've toiled hard, and I lived for the day when I could get a cow. I was left without a husband, my son died in the army, while I worked day and night by the sweat of my brow. The winter nights were so long, but I kept spinning till daylight without rest, so that the tips of my fingers swelled, and I felt as if my eyes were filled with sand. God only knows how bitterly I earned every penny and put them all away until I had saved enough to buy a cow."

"You see, that's what always happens to poor people. Even if

[1] Colloquial for Elias.
[2] Diminutive of Elias.

you work your hands to the very bone, nothing will come of it. That's how it is, so what can you do? Yet one must live somehow."

"My poor, poor head! What am I to do now? Where am I to go for some advice?"

"Try to earn some money to pay for a Mass and then invite those who pray with you to a meal, or go call on St. Ivan Suchavsky. They say he helps a lot."

"I've already done that. I've prayed to the Holy Mother of Zarvanitsia[3] and to Ivan Suchavsky."[4]

"Maybe, as I say, God will help you if you put your trust in Him. May the Lord do the best he can for you."

And Ilash left.

Roman's widow sat beside the cow, giving her as much care as she could to prevent her from dying. She gave her the choicest food she had, but the cow would not eat anything. All she did was look at the old woman, thus causing her more sorrow.

"My dearest one, what's hurting you? Don't leave an old woman without at least a spoonful of milk. Get better and make me a little happy."

And the woman caressed the cow's forehead, the skin under her throat, and lamented over her.

"How can I manage to get another? I can't put the tips of my fingers together, not even to thread a needle. How can I, in my old age, save enough to buy another?"

The cow was shivering and the woman covered her with her sheepskin coat and hovered over her, clad just in her long shirt in the bitter cold. Her teeth chattered, but she would not leave the cow.

"Maybe God is punishing me for my sins? Because many times I've sinned for your sake. Here, I would let you graze along the boundaries of other people's fields; there, I would snatch a small pumpkin for you, or scanty sprigs of cornstalks. But I never begrudged anybody your milk. If I heard that somewhere a child was sick or a woman lying in childbirth, immediately I would hurry there with a cup of milk. I would also give people some cheese for their cornmeal. Lord, don't punish me so hard, me, a poor widow. I won't take anything from others anymore, only spare me this cow."

Thus, till late into the night, Roman's widow wailed over the

[3] A place of pilgrimmage in Western Ukraine.

[4] A Ukrainian saint, venerated in the Province of Bukovina in Western Ukraine.

cow. She sprinkled her with holy water, but nothing helped. The cow stretched her legs across the entire stable and was heaving her flanks with such an effort that the pain of it made her bellow. The old woman petted her, embraced her, spoke to her endearingly, but still could do nothing to ease the animal's suffering.

Through the door the moon lighted the small shed, and the woman saw every movement of the cow. Finally the creature got up. She could hardly stand on her legs. She looked around the stable as if saying goodbye to every nook of it.

Then she fell down on the straw and stretched out as taut as a string on an instrument. The widow knelt down beside her and rubbed her with a wisp of straw. She did not even know what was happening to her. Suddenly the cow bellowed and began to strike out with her legs. The woman's eyes yellowed and she felt a warm glow stream all over her body. Bleeding profusely, she fell to the ground. The cow beat the old widow with her hoofs and began tearing her to pieces.

Both were struggling with death.

C. H. A.

Big News

The news that Hritz[1] Letiuchiy had drowned his little daughter in the river spread through the whole village. He had wanted to drown the older one also, but she had begged him not to. Ever since his wife had died he'd lived in utter poverty. Without her he was helpless, not knowing what to do with the children. Nobody wanted to marry him, and not simply because of the children, but on account of his penury and sheer misery. For two whole years Hritz suffered as he tried to cope alone with his tiny daughters. Nobody knew about him, nobody was aware of how he lived or what he did, except his closest neighbors. They claimed that Hritz did not heat his house most of the winter and that all that

[1] Colloquial for Hrihoriy, Gregory.

time he lay and slept on top of the clay-stove[2] together with his little girls.

And now the entire village began talking about him.

One evening he came home and found his daughters up on the stove.

"Daddy, we want to eat," said Handzia,[3] the older one.

"Then eat me. What can I get you to eat? Look, there's some bread, so help yourselves."

He gave them a large piece of bread, and they began to chew on it like pups on a bare bone.

"She hatched you and then left you for me to worry my head off. I wish the earth would cast her out of itself! The plague must be roaming somewhere – the devil take it! – and it won't drop in on us. Even the plague must be scared of this house."

The daughters did not listen to their father's talk. They heard the same thing every day, every hour, and had grown accustomed to it. Up on top of the stove they ate their bread, and it was pitiful, horrible to look at them. God only knows how those tiny bones held together. Only their four dark eyes looked alive and appeared to weigh anything. It seemed that those eyes might have the weight of lead, while the rest of their bodies, but for them, would have flown away with the wind like feathers. Even now, as they were eating the dry bread, one felt that the bones in their faces would crack up.

Hritz glanced up at them from the bench where he sat, and thought: corpses. He was so frightened at that impression that he was suddenly covered with sweat. Something happened to him, as if a heavy stone had been placed on his chest. The girls were champing the bread, while he fell to the ground and prayed. But he continually felt an urge to glance up at them and think: corpses.

For several days after that Hritz was afraid to stay in the house and never stopped visiting his neighbours. They said that he looked worried. His face grew dark and his eyes sank deep into his head, so that he could hardly see the world around him, and only seemed to look at the stone that weighed heavily on his chest.

One evening Hritz came into the house, boiled a few potatoes, salted them and cast them onto the top of the stove where his children were. When they finished them, he said:

"Get down from there. We're going to visit somebody."

2 See page 27.
3 Diminutive of Anna.

The girls climbed down.

Hritz put ragged shirts on them, took Dotsia,[4] the younger one, in his arms, and Handzia by the hand, and went out of the house with them. For a long time he walked across the meadows and stopped only when he reached the top of a hill. In the moonlight the river in the valley extended before him like a stream of quicksilver. Hritz shuddered, for that sparkling river chilled him, and the stone on his chest became heavier still. He was gasping for breath and could hardly carry little Dotsia.

They began descending toward the river. Hritz was gnashing his teeth so loud that the echo of the sound spread far and wide. On his chest he felt something like a long fiery belt burning his heart and head. On the bank of the river he could not walk slowly; he ran, leaving Handzia behind him. She hurried after him. Suddenly he lifted Dotsia and with all his might threw her into the stream.

He felt relieved and began to speak rapidly:

"I'll tell the officials that there was no other way out. Nothing to eat, nothing to make a fire with, no one to wash clothes or my children's heads. I'll tell them that I am ready for the punishment, because I'm guilty. Then I'll go to the gallows."

Beside him stood Handzia who spoke just as rapidly:

"Daddy, don't drown me, don't drown me, don't drown me!"

"Well, if you're begging so hard, I won't. Still, you'd feel much better there. As for me, it's the same to be punished for one as for two. But you'll find life hard from your early childhood, and then you'll go to serve as a nursemaid to some Jew and suffer even more. But . . . as you like."

"Don't drown me, daddy, please don't!"

"No, no, I won't. But Dotsia will feel much better than you. And now return to the village, while I go and report myself. Here, take this path, continue up and up, and when you come to the first house, go inside and tell them what happened. Say: 'My daddy wanted to drown me, but I begged him not to, and now I'm asking you to let me pass the night here.' And tomorrow, just say: 'Maybe you can help me find a place where I could look after babies!' Now go, because it's night already."

And Handzia went.

"Handzia, Handzia, my dear, here's a small cane for you, because if a dog finds you, he'll tear you up. With a cane you'll be much safer."

4 Colloquial for Eudoxia.

Handzia took the cane and went across the meadows.

Hritz rolled up his pants in order to ford the stream, because in that direction lay his way to the town. He had just stepped into the water, which reached up to his ankles, when suddenly he became rigid.

"In the name of the Father and of the Son and of the Holy Ghost. Amen! Our Father who art in heaven and on earth. . . ."

He turned back and went toward the bridge.

C. H. A.

The Council Meeting

The councillors were slowly gathering in the office. Before entering the house, each one blew his nose in the porch,[1] wiped it with the lap of his sheepskin coat, and used the palms of his hand for the final touches. Having done that, they joined the others. "Glory to Jesus!" was their greeting, to which those present replied: "Forever Be His Glory!" Then each sat on the bench around the walls of the room.

About half of the councillors were already present, the older ones sitting nearer the table, the younger somewhat farther away. In the corner, near the clay-stove, stood straw mattresses piled one on top of the other, and a black tin can alongside. This was a hospital. When, once or twice a year, the doctor wrote to the community that he would be in the village on such and such a day, the reeve summoned the constable, Toma, into his presence.

"Tomorrow, my boy, you'll just have to tidy up the office, because, look here, the letter has just arrived saying that the doctor is coming. You'll scrub the floor a bit, sprinkle it with sand, lay out the straw mattresses on the floor, spill that smelly water out of the can here and there in the corners, and so we'll pull wool

[1] Porch is here used in the sense of an entranceway or hallway which was covered on all sides.

over his eyes. There's a regulation that there's got to be a hospital for cholera, so there's got to be one."

Thus, once or twice a year, the constable turned the office into a hospital. . . . And afterwards, when the councillors came to the meeting, they all sneezed and said: "Phew! It stinks so horribly!" Those who had been in the army said that the doctor must have performed a "reperation" and used some deadening stuff,[2] and it was this that made the nose itch. But Pavlo[3] Dzinio really had it good. He always dozed off at a meeting. And when the councillors sneezed from the hospital odour, they always said:

"Pavlo is soft in the head. We're only sneezing, but he's actually sleeping. We'll have to ask the doctor not to deaden our councillors, or the meeting will be good for nothing."

Pavlo did not defend himself; he only gaped at the councillors with terrified eyes, his face becoming even darker than it was. At the council he was considered as a "substitute for stupidity," and they all laughed at him.

The councillors were now seated on the benches and chatted, slowly, lazily. Each sat the way he liked best, in a position to which he was accustomed. Ivan Plaviuk, who was sitting right by the table and was the oldest, lowered his head over his belly, folded his hands as if in prayer, stuck them between his knees, and kept spitting as he puffed away at his pipe. The palms of his hands, nose and knees were in the neighborhood of each other. Thus he sat and spoke about the market conditions.

"Don't even talk to me about the kind of markets we have today. The Jews together with the landlords have taken over the whole world. Who sells? The Jews. And who buys? The landlords. And the common run of people sell some larger animals only now and then. A cow or a calf they sell occasionally, but oxen – very seldom."

"Things are sure tight! Everyone thinks: 'I'll buy a calf, look after it for a while, steam a dash of chaff for it from time to time, toss it a few pumpkins and, for all you know, something will be gained to take care of a few minor expenses.' Tight years are really upon us!"

"True enough, they're tight. In the distant past, the priests used to holler that people shouldn't drink, shouldn't live loosely and wastefully, but now, do you see, people don't drink, don't

2 Anaesthetic.
3 Paul.

fritter anything away and never see a penny anyway. People are up against the wall alright, and hardly anyone has any salted pork at Easter. I'm telling you, to come by a penny nowadays is as hard as squeezing it out of a stone."

"Everything has changed completely. Why, long ago you didn't even see this kind of cattle. These days the cattle are all piebald – Tyrolese. Years ago they were all white. I haven't been a land-holder for too long a time yet, but in my wife's dowry I got oxen white as snow, with horns so long that they could hardly squeeze through the gate. They used to run like horses. And whenever I drove to town, I bridled them with bits. People said they were Hungarian cattle, as they now say that the present kind are sup-posed to be Tyrolese. And were the cattle cheap then, ho-ho-ho!"

"Things were sold cheap and were bought cheap, but the times were certainly better. Look here, it's not only the cattle that are different today. How about the pigs – were they the same long ago? They were, you know, of every color, with long bristles and leggy. Today they're all white and smooth. So when you stand at a pig market, it's filled with them, and they all seem to be covered as if with white blossoms. Only pot-bellied Mazurians[4] wander among them."

"It seems there's every kind. And people aren't the same either. The other day I was in Kolomiya and, as I looked around, I saw something like a devil walking about – may God forgive me! His face was all black, and the hands too. I thought to myself: 'If this fellow ever stood on a bridge at night, everyone would have to have the water blessed!' Some Jewish guy was saying that there are people like that under the sun."

"It's a sure thing that there are all sorts of them. When my Vasyl[5] was in the army in Vienna, he said he saw the kind of pigs on which you can see neither ears, nor snouts, nor legs, only their torsos."

"There's everything in the world, but of misery there's the most. . . ."

The conversation ceased, because the reeve walked in.

"What's the news in town, reeve?"

"If there was any money, things would be alright in town," said the reeve. "When the rich walk into a restaurant, they eat and drink the very best, and they still have money. If only for a week I could turn into such a rich gentleman!"

4 Mazuria, northeastern region of Poland.
5 Basil.

"It depends into what kind of a rich gentleman! Because there are some that sleep in the straw and scratch for lice with their teeth. One like that has a vest on, but no shirt. Why, he lays a bit of cloth on his breast, and pretends he's dressed! And many of those characters are so hungry that they'd eat even an oil-cake."

This observation was made by Protz[6] who, some time ago, had served in a manor house.

"I was at the secretary's about that pastureland again. He muttered some nonsense to me there. 'If only people in your village ordered fewer of those newspapers at the post office! It's a swindle,' he said. 'It looks like muzhiks are very plentiful, and if only one in twenty gives a *lev* for the paper, it adds up to thousands upon thousands of money wasted, all for nothing. Some gent writes all sorts of things himself, invents a lot of humbug, glosses it over, smooths it out, and the crazy muzhiks,' he said, 'just lap it up and smack their lips at the idea that the landlords' fields are to be turned over to the people.' "

"And you must have stood there and yes-yessed him, didn't you?" inquired a young councillor, Petro[7] Antoniv.

"Of course, you would expect me to grab him by the shoulders and have a scuffle over some scoundrel who befuddles people! A priest from Hrusheva spoke the truth when he said that people allow themselves to be stirred up by all kinds of criminals, and then, when the jig is up, the culprits skip out and the foolish people are put in jails. Why, haven't enough of them been injured and crippled? Only I don't like it when someone gives me a dig. As if I'd sold out or betrayed the community; as if I was pushing to get myself elected. Elect whoever you want. I'll stand aside."

"You sure would push yourself, but we say: shoo! You'd even try to bribe kids by bringing sausages right to their homes," retorted Petro Antoniv.

"Shut up!" shouted the reeve. "Shut up, or I'll order you to be handcuffed, you snotter. Look here, fellow-members, do you think that I ever herded swine with this punk?"

"You never wiped my nose, and you can yes-yes me for what I say just as you yes-yessed the secretary."

The quarrel was beginning to turn into a fight, and old Ivan had to intervene.

"Petro, my boy, don't be stubborn. You know very well that a younger man must hold his tongue in front of the older folk. One

6 Colloquial for Procopius.
7 Peter.

55

man is such that he fears nothing, while the next fellow is scared. I myself, fellow-landowners, have always stood and still stand for the community, but, honest to goodness, I'd never go to your general meeting. I happened to be in the city last fall. A forester came up to me and said: 'Come to the meeting and, at least in your old age, see how the muzhiks are banding together.' I told him: 'By God, I won't go! It's a good thing they're uniting, because, as the saying goes, "community is a big man", but I won't go. I've grown up and lived to become hoary,' said I, 'but I haven't been in jail even an hour. And am I to dishonour my old age now?' Why, it seems to me that every little child in the village would point at me and say: 'Look, there's uncle Ivan, and he's been in jail!' I won't go, and never will. My Mykola goes, but I won't."

Somehow, by saying this and that, old Ivan halted the quarrel. But the angry feelings remained unabated.

"But we just talk, and you, reeve, aren't telling us why you called us here," said Ivan in order to prevent the quarrel from breaking out again.

"I won't be calling you again. If only I last out my term, I'll spit on the office, and let the snotters be your reeves."

"My, my, so you think we won't find a reeve? We could supply the whole district with reeves from our village," retorted Petro unforgivingly.

"Well, the church elder has something to say to the council," said the reeve.

The church elder, Vasyl, began to speak:

"Let's see, I don't remember whether it was Thursday or Friday when the secretary's lad came running to me. 'Oh, uncle,' he said, 'I saw Roman's old widow carrying a board away from under the church.' The next day I went to the church, and, sure enough, one board wasn't there. It was one of those that were left over from the belfry. It's true, those boards are pretty well rotted, but to steal them from under the church is a different matter. You see, she's an old woman and ought to know better than to carry away what's not hers. I went to the priest and told him the whole story. And the priest said that the council must be told about this, because, as he said, it wouldn't do to steal from the church. I myself wouldn't give a hoot if the thing was mine, but it belongs to the church and must be protected," concluded Vasyl accusingly.

All the councillors sat silent, for who would have expected

Roman's old widow to be a thief? It had never been even rumoured in the village that she had ever stolen anything.

In a while Roman's widow appeared. She was old, tattered, and her face was blue. Standing by the door, she began speaking rapidly, through tears:

"I, councillors, did indeed steal that board. I stole it so that you might know how my son takes care of me in my old age. I haven't a wisp of straw in the house, not enough even to make some smoke with. I'm sitting on the clay-stove[8] and freezing. I sew and spin for the whole village, and my fingers are turning stiff and numb, like wood. My eyes are all bleary. I can still sew enough to keep body and soul together, but there isn't a penny for fuel. And I gave my son what little land I had and left myself only a hut to live in, and he won't pop in to see me at least once a month. If he'd only drop in and say: 'Satan, or Devil, how are you doing?' But no, never."

"But to steal from under the church!? Why, woman, you're not long for this world, and you must remember that you're to take something good with you to the other side. You're an old woman, and, for that reason, I declare that you're not to be locked up or beaten. You'll only give a lev[9] to the church. Then you may go your way with God, and let me hear no more of any thieving."

Such was the reeve's judgment.

"Oh, my dear reeve, I'll die and never see a lev! Where am I to get a lev, where, where, where?"

"You must!" was the reply.

The councillors were silent. They knew that the woman was very hard up and had no lev. But she had stolen, and what's true is true; and what's more, from the church! They were on the verge of suggesting that she pay a little at a time, a penny now and a penny then, when Petro Antoniv spoke up:

"People, I would say that we ought not to punish such a poor widow. The church probably won't be enriched by one lev from her. Somewhere it has been said that long ago churches sank into the earth, and in their places bottomless lakes appeared. Were all such widows' bitterly earned levs gathered and placed in the churches' coffers, no church would likely hold within itself all the widows' tears. I am sure this wouldn't be right. Instead of the church giving something to the old woman, should it, on the

8 See page 27.
9 Rumanian currency, usually a gold coin.

other hand, take from her that miserable cold *lev*? The other day I went to her place for some unspun hemp. I went in, and her house was colder than any landholder's stable. On top of the oven burned a lampwick the size of a wheat kernel. And that's all the fire there was in the house. The woman sat and rubbed her fingers which were as hard as wood. I'd say, councillors, that we shouldn't ask her to pay that *lev*."

The reeve looked angrily at Petro. The councillors felt as if a stone had fallen off their hearts. They all spoke out at once and agreed that the woman's *lev* need not be taken. And old Ivan said: "May God forbid that it should be!"

They also ordered that her son be called before them. When he appeared, it was old Ivan who proceeded to upbraid him:

"You! You! To think how she cared for you in your infancy, and sought cool shelter for you under a bush, while she worked in the field! How she washed and patched your clothes, and wept when you were drafted into military service! And now you won't toss her way a wisp of straw? Ah! How I wish I was the reeve! I'd have you chained up and around to the very last link."

That was what Ivan said with much authority.

Children

He put the rake beside himself, sat down on the boundary line, lit his pipe and, as thoughts clashed in his mind, he shouted loud enough to be heard many fields away.

"Just let me get a bit of peaceful rest here, because as soon as I appear, they find some work for the old man. Even my daughter-in-law — I wish her no harm — the minute she spies me, screams out: 'Don't just sit there, do something.'

"Why, the Lord above us sees that I can hardly drag my feet along. And my hands are like worn-out scrapers. For a whole month I haven't shaved. And I've forgotten the road to the church. How can I go there without decent clothes? They've taken everything off my back."

Along the boundary line and across the entire field roamed the old man's voice. All the people around turned in his direction. Meanwhile he continued to complain:

"Oh, such are the children these days! But, thank God, I still have my wits about me. I still remember the talk we had at the notary's office. He was a skimpy gentleman with a scanty beard. And it was he who explained the matter to my son. He said: 'As long as he's alive, he must have the bed; he must sleep in it and lie in it even till sunrise if he likes. But,' he said, 'when you put him on the bench[1] and then burrow him into the earth, you may move from the bench to the old man's bed. And the old woman, too, must have her own place on top of the stove,[2] so that she can keep warm and pray there. But when you wash her body and place her hands crosswise,[3] then let the daughter-in-law climb to the top of the stove, because only then will that space belong to her.'"

The autumn wind played with the old man's grey hair.

"If only some night the notary would come and look into the house! The son lies in the bed, the daughter-in-law on top of the stove, and my old wife and I are grovelling on the floor, on the straw. Is that right? and where is God? He's not among people like that, oh no!"

Even with his head he gestured that young people have no God in them.

"You old ones might as well croak; not a spoonful of food can be spared for you. They drink fresh milk, eat tasty cheese, while we look at them like pups. And to think! I've given them the cow, a few sheep, the plow; all I had I've given them. Just as other people give, so did I. But now they tell me: 'You're pretty old and feeble; you must eat less.' That's what our children tell us."

The old man's voice faltered and he cut short his speech.

"They'll even bury us like dogs. By God! They won't even put the boots on our feet."

A flock of storks suddenly descended upon the reeds, flapping their wings above the old man so loudly that he became frightened. They were getting ready to fly away to warmer climes.

"So the fall is here already! And just as soon Christmas is sure to come.

"They're only birds, but imagine how clever they are! Only they can't talk. But as soon as they feel something bothering them,

1 When he dies, and is laid out on the bench, as on a bier.
2 See page 27.
3 After she dies.

they try to make it better for themselves. In winter there are no frogs, and it's cold. And that's what they know in advance. They're not like a man who has to linger in the same spot for the rest of his short life."

He arose from the boundary line, hid his pipe, picked up the rake and started out homeward. Several times he turned to look at the storks. Then he stopped.

"I wonder if some kind man could tell me whether my old wife and I will live long enough to see them again when they return? Maybe one of us will pop off, or maybe neither of us will see the storks at all. . . ."

C. H. A.

The Signature

Little Dotsia[1] was walking back and forth on the bench behind the shoulders of the landholders who were seated at a long table, learning to write their names. Each one had a written copy of his name. With heavy hands these scribblers were examining their copies from every side in order to find where it would be the easiest for them to begin. They pressed their chests against the table so hard that it creaked. The learning proceeded very quietly. Only the smacking of lips was heard as the men moistened the pencils in their mouths. Blonde-headed Dotsia watched each one of them to see whether he wrote correctly.

"Well, Dotsia, come and see. How does it look?"

"It's still as messy and rough as unbrushed yarn. Write it again."

And the landowner shoved the tip of the pencil into his mouth and tried once more.

"Now, come and glance at mine, because I've been scratching it for two evenings until my chest aches. Come and read what I have written."

[1] Colloquial for Eudoxia.

"Pavlo[2] Lazirenko."

"That's me, exactly. Is it there so that everyone can see who it is?"

"Anyone who is educated enough."

Pavlo blushed with delight and viewed the little card from every angle.

"Well, I'm going to copy it once more."

He leaned forward and moistened the tip of his pencil with his saliva.

Dotsia was walking behind the shoulders of the landholders in a somewhat sedate manner. Her mother was looking at the scene from the top of the clay-stove[3] and kept the boys quiet, preventing them from screaming for fear that the men might muddle their letters.

On the bench sat old Yakiv[4] Yaremiv and with much satisfaction watched the process of that instruction. Finally, he could no longer resist and had to speak out. For two hours he had been looking on with the greatest attention. Now his patience snapped.

"Listen, fellows, leave some of it for tomorrow. If you don't, your chests will crack."

His well-to-do friends raised their heads and looked dumbfounded.

"It was I who discovered this good fortune for you, and you must thank me for it. And you must each buy a present for Dotsia."

"Tell us, what was it that put such a thought into your head?"

"Hard knocks gave me that advice."

"What hard knocks?"

"Promissory notes."

And for the hundredth time old Yakiv began to relate how it happened.

"Of course, you all know that I didn't tie up my land in the bank to buy whiskey, or God would have punished me for it. It was my old woman who set me up to it."

"How did she?"

"My, my! You fellows are young and, as I see, you're learning to write, and still you don't know anything. Once it happened that she came out of the storage room and said: 'Listen, old man, there's no flour in the sack, just about two small bowlsful.' I thought about it for a long while, and then started out to town to

2 Paul.
3 See page 27.
4 Jacob, James.

apply for a loan of a hundred *levs*[5] from the bank which advances money on one's future crops.

"You see, I came to that bank and stated my case. I said: 'There's no bread for the children, so I beg you, sir, if it may please God's grace and yours, lend me a hundred *levs*.' "

—[6] "Have you any land?"

— "I have sir. These days, if you have no land, no one will give you any money, that I know."

— "Is it in your name?"

— "It is."

— "Is the title to it clear?"

— "Every bit of it is clear."

— "Have you any debts?"

— "Well, somewhere among the Jews I have a little debt, no greater than a tiny scab. But with this hundred I'll be able to toss some bread to the children and stop the Jews from yelping."

— "Then bring the title and the document on which your debt is stated. After that there will be a meeting."

— "And when am I to come to that meeting?"

— "Just try to reason with a muzhik! You're not needed at the meeting, just bring the papers."

— "Pardon me, sir. I didn't understand. The papers are right here."

"I took them out of my shirt and handed them to him. 'Here they are,' I said. 'Everything is there somewhere, because I put things together, all the letters I receive. You see, I don't understand what's in them, so I keep them all together.' He picked through them, found what he was after, and said: 'Come in a week's time.'

"I went there about three times, and at last he told me that the loan was approved."

— "Can you write, old man?"

— "Too bad, I can't, sir. I didn't go to school, wasn't in the army, so I'm completely ignorant."

— "Then you'll have to sign the note before a notary."

— "If you please, I'll make a mark with my own hand, just a little cross, and you will sign for me."

— "It's not permitted," he said, "to put crosses on promissory notes."

[5] Monetary unit, usually a gold coin, used in that part of the country.
[6] The dashes are used to indicate that the speaker is relating a conversation.

"And there I stood, thinking: 'Now, if they deduct something for entering my mortgage in their books, take the interest in advance, and pay the notary, there won't be much of that capital left for me.'

"I scurried about the town for guarantors and came across a shoemaker, that thief Lapchinsky. The wretch is always roaming about the town. I stopped him and began telling him about my trouble."

— "The muzhik," he said, "is always a fool. All winter long he decays indoors and doesn't even learn how to put his family name down in writing."

— "Although you're an out-and-out thief, and a swill-carrier for the Jews, your words make sense," I thought to myself and hurried on.

"I brought the guarantors, and they signed for me before a notary. But thirteen *levs* were cut out of my hundred.

"As I was taking the money home, that shoemaker stayed in my mind. What if he is a thief? The words he speaks are worth hearing. Just imagine, they strip your skin, removing it as off an ox. A hundred you're supposed to have borrowed, and what are you taking home?"

Whenever he reached this point, Yakiv would always spit. He did so now.

"Everyone wants to take, everyone wants something for nothing; and in the meantime everything has become as tight as tight can be.

"I put the money in the chest and said to Dotsia: 'Listen, my dear, teach your grandpa to sign his name, so that he wouldn't be stuffing the throats of the rich, because they are already stuffed enough. I'd rather buy a kerchief for you.'

"And she did teach me. You heard about it in the village and laughed at the old man. But when you found yourselves in a tight fix and had to sign promissory notes, you followed the old man to Dotsia. I showed you the way, and now you won't be losing money."

"Well, now we won't," replied the landholders. "And we have to thank you and our teacher Dotsia for that."

"But each one of you must bring her a present."

"Of course, we will."

Dotsia sat on top of the clay-stove and was overjoyed. Her mother smiled at her proudly.

Days Gone By

All three of them are already in their tombs. For quite some time now the cherry trees have blossomed and borne fruit above their graves, and the oak crosses at their heads are leaning from age. They died long ago: old Dmitro[1], his wife, and the precentor,[2] Bazio.

Old Dmitro settled his four sons on the land. And when he settled them, he was left in a time-worn house, alone with his aged wife. Not only with his wife, but also with oxen, a cow, and several acres of land. He worked about the yard and tended the oxen, and his wife busied herself in the house; the sons sowed the fields which were later harvested by poor people who received every third sheaf as their wages. The old man took care of the oxen, watered and brushed them, swept the barn and the yard, and cut down the thistles along the interwoven fence. But his foremost occupation came from his habit of climbing up into the barn loft and there rummaging about old plows, harrows, small wagon-ladders, and yokes. No small number of wooden things had accumulated during his fifty years as a landowner. And he always threw something down from the loft to the ground and dragged it to the lawn in front of the house. He examined, tested and mended it all. That was his most cherished pursuit. No doubt, in so doing, he used to recall the years gone by when he worked with these implements, and that is why what he did was so much pleasure. When he was not brushing the oxen, he was sure to be working away at an old yoke or some ancient plow.

He fed the oxen for three years. After three years he drove them into town to market. He received four hundred *rinskis*[3] for them; for two hundred he bought another yoke of young oxen, and hid the remaining two hundred in an old tax-book and locked it away in the chest.

He hadn't threshed grain for about a dozen years, and his yard was surrounded by stacks. The oldest stack was black, the next one grey, another, smaller than the previous one, light grey, that of the preceding fall was white, and the current year's yield as yellow as wax.

1 Colloquial for Demetrius.
2 Church cantor.
3 Austrian currency.

Every month he examined the stacks to see whether they had been gnawed by mice or become musty. He would pull out a handful of stalks from each one, smell it, and look to see whether the heads shredded or not. If it became necessary to have one of them threshed, he summond the threshers. Then again he hid the money gained from it in the tax-book and locked the chest with a padlock.

He attended church every other Sunday, alternating with his wife. She went to the holy service on the first feast of the Mother of God,[4] and he on the second;[5] she at Easter and he at Christmas. On his Sunday he would climb into the house attic and throw large and little boots into the porch.[6] The large ones were his. He wore them as a young man, when he was married, and during his early years as a landowner; the smaller ones were those which his sons had worn while they were growing up in his home. He would sit down on the prizba,[7] put those boots on it, rub them with a dust-cloth, and smear them with tar-oil. He selected a pair to wear to church and placed the others in a row, out in the sun, so that the oil might penetrate the leather. Then he instructed his wife not only to brush the oxen, but also keep an eye on the boots, so that no dog would carry any of them away. In church he devotedly bowed his head to the floor many times,[8] placed mouldy kreutzers on the offering-plate and, perspiring, came out along with the others.

"Grandpa, you'll forget to talk," some of them would say to him.

"My generation had died out or perished in the wars. I haven't anyone to talk with."

When he returned home, he ate bread with garlic or, except on fast days and during Lent, salted pork. There were three barrels of salted pork in the larder. In one, the pork was three years old, yellow and soft as butter. This was grandpa's barrel. In the second, two-year-old one, the pork was half yellow and half white. It belonged to his wife. In the third, the current year's pork was white as paper. This one was the children's barrel, because they

4 The Assumption of the Virgin, August 15.
5 The Nativity of the Virgin, September 8.
6 A small covered hallway at the entrance to a cottage.
7 A clay ledge about a foot in height and width, adjacent to the foundation of a peasant's home. It deflected rain and was often used as a bench to sit on.
8 Deep genuflections.

liked only fresh salted pork. After the meal Dmitro would go out to look at the oxen. Having done that, he would throw the big and little boots back into the attic and go to sleep under the cherry tree. In this manner his days followed one another, peacefully and calmly. His teeth never ached, nor was he racked by any kind of illness, and in all his life he never had a sorceress near him.

Dmitro's wife was more of a fiery than tender feminine nature. She just liked to talk and to start endless conversations without which she could neither eat nor sleep. She did not even come near her husband. He was always silent, and if she wanted to say only a word or two to him, he would drop the old harrow or axle and slip away from her.

"That old clumsy dolt thinks I'm going to kiss him or something."

She would spit in disgust and go to the gate or to the pond in search of women eager for chatter. Then the old man returned to his work, mumbling under his nose:

"It's plain to see that she's aged. Her face is like leather on an old boot, and her hair is white as milk, but her tongue has not aged a bit. With it she could grind a hundred bushels a day and still look around to see if there wasn't another hundred."

God had not given grandma a daughter. In her younger years she had always hoped for a daughter, and had prepared a dowry for her. But God had not given her one, and now she had woven and sewn so much that the clothes-poles supporting the linens and rugs were just sagging. More than once grandpa asked in anger for whom she was sewing and weaving so many rags.

"Go away, old man, go away and don't bother me about that, or I'll take all your worm-eaten junk out of the attic and throw it into the fire. Just you dare touch my clothes-poles, and you won't even see me pile your plows and wagons and toss them all into the oven."

Grandpa would cringe like a sparrow and rush away from her, for how could he win out against her? Meanwhile grandma would seat herself in front of the clothes-poles and talk to herself:

"In each section of the clothes-poles there is the same amount of everything, there, and there, and there. Every daughter-in-law may take either this one or that one, because everyone of them is the same. But the fifth one is to go to the church, for my husband and me.[9] This one is not to be touched by any daughter-in-law of mine, or I'll cut off her hands."

[9] For Masses or commemorative services for the deceased.

On Sunday afternoon all the daughters-in-law came to visit grandma, along with her grandchildren. They were as beautiful as marigolds, with faces as red as cranberries. Grandma seated them at the table, served them the current year's salted pork, and talked with them, cackling like a hen among her chicks:

"When I die, each one of you is to take one section on the clothes-pole, because each one of them is the same, just as you are all alike to me, my children. But if grandpa should die after I do, don't any of you dare touch a thread of it. He would grieve so much for them that he would drop dead on the spot. Also be sure to warn your husbands not to take the smallest thing from his attic, because he's so much in love with it that he couldn't be without it for a day. It would kill him if they did. May the Lord prevent that! And when I die, the four of you are to lament over me with wonderful voices and beautiful words. Also when grandpa dies, you are to lament for him with still more beautiful voices, and even more wonderful words. He will leave you money, so much that you will be able to play with it."

Grandma wept, and the daughters-in-law wept also. Then she kissed each one of them and led them into the other room to show them the rugs. In the yard the grandchildren played with grandpa. They had each got an apple or a bun from grandma, and were looking intently at an old maple yoke. Grandpa was showing them the carvings of plows, oxen and drivers on the yoke and telling them that before long they, too, would be going into the fields to plow.

When the sun was setting the daughters-in-law with the children would start out for home. Grandma would accompany them past the gate and there continue talking with them for a long while yet.

The third one among them was the precentor, Bazio. He was neither kith nor kin to them, but he lived just across the garden from them. Dmitro's wife always carried meals to him, for he was old and lived alone. But, perhaps, he never ate grandma's meals, because he was always drunk.

"Bazio, why do you drink so much whiskey? I'm telling you, some day it's going to catch fire inside you."

"My dear crony, how am I not to drink when books, like rabbits, are running around in my head? Every verse, every tittle thrusts itself forward to be sung or read, until my head is just splitting apart. Like a countless number of small children, they want to barge through one narrow door and make themselves heard. My head is so small, and close-cropped at that, so where am I to put them? It's all very well that you have settled your children on plots of land, but mine are all in a heap. That's why I have to fill them up with whiskey, so that they will all get drunk and give me a little peace."

Grandma kept shaking her head apprehensively.

"My! How terrible learning must be! It's not like swinging a flail."

But again she would give Bazio money for whiskey. To repay her, he would come to grandma's house on many a Sunday and read humorous pamphlets. The sons and daughters-in-laws almost died laughing at Lutz Zalivayko[10] and at the turkey which had only as much sense as was in his tail.

But on one occasion Bazio read them such a terrifying booklet that grandma and her daughters-in-law burst into tears from fright, and the sons became quite gloomy.

"The earth shall not bring forth her fruit, and I shall send a plague upon your cattle and they shall die; and I shall drown your people. Rains shall not descend upon the earth, and the earth shall be like stone, and will not cause any growth to spring forth. . . ."

Bazio himself felt that he had gone a bit too far, and found the following words in that book:

"Whoever has this *Letter* on him, or reads it often, or humbly listens to it, or copies it, shall find favor with God. . . . In whichever home this *Letter* is to be found, there neither fire, nor water, nor thunder, nor any evil thing shall be able to harm it."

To some extent this raised the spirits of Bazio, grandma and the daughters-in-law. They at once gave the precentor money to buy them that book. All the women in the village followed grandma's example and gave the precentor money so that their homes, too, would be insured against fire and lightning. He bought them the books, and for himself, while he was at it, a woolen topcoat and a new porcelain pipe. After that, every Sunday, he read the book in different women's homes, and charged them twenty kreutzers each for whiskey and a plaited bread besides, so as to provide himself with a snack.

There were only a few homes left in which Bazio had not done any reading, just several poor dwellings near the woods, when he

10 A humorous drunkard in the book of the same name.

became ill. He was seized with the shivers, then lapsed into fever. After that, some people said, a tiny flame issued from his mouth and Bazio gave up his soul to God. Perhaps the whiskey inside him had ignited. Suffice it to say that all the women wept and lamented over him as if he were their own brother.

Dmitro's old wife did not grieve long, for in the autumn she, too, followed the precentor on that distant journey. Grandpa Dmitro likewise did not linger long without her, and in the spring wended his way to the grave.

People forgot about them long ago because it was not recently that they died. Only the members of the Reading Room[11] in the village mention them now and then when they happen to reminisce about its beginnings.

"The actual beginning of the Reading Room dates back to old Dmitro, his wife, and the precentor Bazio. It was in their home that the precentor for the first time began to read his pamphlets. Even now, copies of "God's Letter" and those of "Lutz Zalivayko" are to be found tucked away somewhere under the ceiling-beams. But now no one reads them anymore. Their time has passed away."

"Alas, their time has passed away."

"And those three kinds of salted pork have also passed away."

"Too bad! You couldn't overtake them even with a horse!"

May

Danilo[1] waited by the white gate, looking into the squire's garden like a thief, but not daring to enter.

"How should I know if one is allowed to go in there? What if he comes rushing out and smacks me in the mug? How should I know that he wouldn't?"

---

[11] A society established for illiterate peasants. There they were read books and newspapers.
[1] Colloquial for Danyil, Daniel.

The paths across the squire's garden were spotlessly clean and even. It was on account of them that he was afraid of a beating, because it was only by walking down them that one was able to get to the courtyard. In the meantime he waited by the gate.

All the muzhiks, many millions of them, know how to wait long and patiently. When the squire is in his office, they stand and wait. No matter how many of them there are, they will not let the slightest sound of life be heard. They stand silently, their features gradually become rigid, and the expressions on their faces slip somewhere down to their shoulders, under their shirts. In that erect drowsiness they are only half conscious of themselves and altogether indifferent, while the official appears among them like a black fly which has crawled into thick honey. The one at the head, who is the closest to the office table, feels the worst, because he cannot fall into real sleep. At every moment he rounds out his eyes, widening them so much that they seem to reach under the mop of his hair, and looks around himself with anxiety. Behind him his neighbors must keep their eyes well peeled, and the anxiety of the one at the head storms across them all. That first one is like the wind in the field, continually making restless the ears of wheat, from the road up to the very ridge.

If the squire is not in his office, then they sit down on the floor. They find it so pleasant to rest at least for a half hour, so very pleasant to relax at least one of their hands or feet. They crowd together, and each lets a particular part of his body get a brief respite. Some hold their hats carefully, so as not to crumple them, and when they have pressed themselves really close together, they begin to speak in whispers:

"If only I could get a few puffs from my pipe."

"Forget it."

"Did you buy your tobacco?"[2]

"No, it grows in my own garden."

"Don't speak so loud, someone might hear you, and then. . . ."

After that they all shove their hands inside their shirts and push their rolled pouches around from their chests and down their backs for fear that some wretch of an inspector might search them. The whispers subside, the faces grow wooden, saliva trickles through their lips, and their heads fall on their chests. And if among them there happens to be one who is impatient, then he, like the one at the head, will not let those sitting on the floor rest

[2] Tobacco growing and selling was the monopoly of the state.

peacefully; because either his hand becomes numb or some misery stings his back so painfully that he is not able to stand it and must make a move. He sets his neighbors all astir and, in a chain reaction, all the harmony of the crowd's support is lost. There begin different posturings of hands and feet until some nuisance again destroys the new configurations.

"Dear Lord! How impatient some people are!" someone who can bear it all says and immediately closes his eyes.

So they all wait. So did Danilo wait by the gate, although he was alone. Drowsiness and indifference fell upon him and his thoughts became intermingled. When he was on the way to the squire's place, he had a very clear plan: on seeing him, he would take off his hat and approach him directly, like a stork walking on a marsh – carefully, lightly, so as not to jar a single pebble. When he had drawn quite close to him, he would open his eyes wide and stare at the squire so as to make him think: 'This one must really be poor.' Then he would step up to him, take his hand, kiss it on both sides, apply his forehead to the squire's palm and move slightly back. Having done that, he would lower his shoulders, cast his hat on the ground behind him, wipe his lips with his sleeve and begin to speak:

"I came to your lordship to beg you to hire me. I find the time before the harvest very harsh. I have four children, and there is only a small patch of garden from which to feed them. I must hire myself out. I can do any kind of work, because I'm a man used to all sorts of labour. And so I beg God's and your lordship's grace that we may come to some agreement, so that I can get a hundred kilograms of produce even now for my wife to feed the children. As for me, I can start work at once."

The squire's first question might well be:

"You must be a thief."

"Your lordship, I haven't stolen a blade of grass belonging to others."

"Why do you lie, you scoundrel? It's impossible for a muzhik not to steal. You are a muzhik, aren't you?"

"I'm a common, ordinary muzhik, but I don't like to take what's not mine."

"Then you must be a drunkard."

"Whiskey and I don't go together, because I can't afford it."

"You lie. Why, you would die if you didn't have any whiskey."

"Without whiskey one wouldn't die, but without bread one might."

"You're clever in your replies, because you were in prison, and there they pounded some sense into your head."

"God forbid! I've lived to become a middle-aged man, and yet my foot had never been in prison."

"And why have you produced so many children?"

"Your lordship, it's God who gives children."

"Has the priest taught you that?"

"I have nothing to do with the priest, because that costs money; and I don't go to church because I haven't decent clothes to put on."

"So you're a radical and won't let the priest skin you?"

"Even if I wanted to give the priest something, I couldn't, because I have nothing to give; and even if he wanted to skin me, he couldn't, because there's nothing to skin. We just don't get together."

He knew in advance that first of all the squire had to make a man wallow in the mud, have fun at his expense, and only then would he hire him. On his way, he was sure of himself until he reached the gate and leaned on it. This manor happened to be in another village, and he did not know how one gets inside it. In addition, it was out in the fields, and there was no one around to ask for the directions. So Danilo waited. His clear plan was becoming tarnished. He scratched his neck and timidly looked into the garden.

"They must take walks down those paths, because the whole course is packed with fine sand."

His eyes wandered about for a long time until they were arrested by the peacock which sparkled in front of the manor-house.

"I could get a pretty penny for that tail if I could only get my hands into it. . . I wonder if the bird's meat is good to eat?"

He looked around to see the cottages.

"This man has quite a bit of land, and works it well to produce so much bread. What on earth does he do with it all?"

His thoughts were scattered in all directions.

"The spring is so nice, so nice that I can't even say how fine it is."

As time passed, he did not notice anything else. He sat rigid and felt that he would soon fall asleep. To prevent that, he kept his eyes wide open, rubbed his face with his hands, and looked like an unfortunate wrestler who at any moment now would give himself up to the mercy or harshness of his enemy. In a short while he leaned to one side and, it appeared, wanted to place himself in such a manner that he would sleep and yet seem to be waiting. Then he stretched himself out altogether and closed his eyes. He hadn't slept a moment when something whispered to him:

"Sleep, sleep right by the squire's gate, and the wagoner will come along and slash you with his whip so hard that your blood will spurt out."

He sprang to his feet, very frightened, and stood looking around himself as if he were wounded by a shot. He stood thus for a second. Then he waved his hand in a gesture of resignation, walked toward to meadow, crawled into the tall grass and stretched himself out to have a sound sleep. As he was drowsing off he seemed to envision the squire, his hands, and the fine paths. The squire told him to put his hat on, but he would not.

"May it please your lordship, I'm a poor man, I cannot put the hat on my head in front of you, because I'm a poor man, such a poor man. . . ."

His deep sleep drove those visions away and he slept peacefully.

The sun laughed out loud above him, sent its rays to him, fondled him as his own dear mother would. The flowers kissed his black uncombed hair, and the grass-hoppers leaped over him. And as he slept so calmly, his dark legs and arms looked as if they were moulded into his brick-brown body.

C. H. A.

The Arsonist

Andriy Kurochka, the rich man of the village, sat at the table having his noonday meal. He did not eat but choked on every piece he put into his mouth. His domestic servants came into the house, brought in muddied basins, quarrelled, bustled about and carried them out to place them among the cattle. The children and servants of this wealthy peasant were dirty and lean. Upon them they bore the crude and heavy yoke of the muzhik's riches which never afford any peace or happiness. The rich man grew weary in that yoke more than anybody else, cursed his destiny and endlessly drove his children and hired hands to do more work.

Beside him, on the bench under the window, sat his field-worker of many years' standing, old Fedir.[1]

"I never get that happy moment when I could devour a chunk of bread in peace. I rush and beat about, and one of these days you'll see me drop down and croak. And how can I eat this meal with any pleasure when I know that, without me in the barn, they're not working at all. All they want is to gorge themselves and knock off for the day. What can I say of the others when my own children don't want to work! By God, I don't know how those people of mine will live. After I'm gone, they will all become beggars."

He gobbled the food in such haste that his eyes bulged out.

"And why did you drop in, Fedir?"

"Do you think I would drop in if I was well off? The winter is coming and I haven't a thing to put on my bare feet. Give me two *levs*.[2] I'll repay them by working for you."

"But are you able to work? Your working days are finished, Fedir."

"Well, even if I don't work, you could at least give me a meal for nothing."

"That won't be! These days one doesn't eat for doing nothing. And even if one does some work, he doesn't deserve to eat, the work is so bad! Haven't I asked you to let me hire your girl? You would have had money now."

"But she didn't want to. She went to serve in the manor."

"Of course. The one who doesn't want to work shoves himself into the manor, because there, even if you're given little to eat, at least you can idle your time away. There are some people nowadays that as long as they eat only once a day, and do nothing, think they're in heaven. They get as much as they work for, as much of God's blessing as they deserve. To get ahead now one has to work so hard that he becomes as lean as a string. Well, I'll give you two *levs*, but don't come begging for more. And don't even complain, because I won't give you more. You see yourself that your work in worthless."

"But I must go to people for help, Andriy.[3] What am I to do with myself?"

[1] Colloquial for Theodore.
[2] A Rumanian monetary denomination.
[3] Andrew.

"Do what you like with yourself, but you're no longer fit to associate with those who are well-to-do. Find yourself something to do at the Jew's place or at the landlord's. The work there is easier."

"That's fine advice you've giving me! After I've lost all my strength working for you, now, in my old age, I'm to do mean jobs for the Jews?"

"You haven't worked for me for nothing."

"Let's leave it at that. Goodbye."

And Fedir went out of the house.

"Those beggars would certainly like to take everything from me! Such a coughing, slobbering creature that's not strong enough to hold a flail in his hands, and yet he's trying to put on airs! Go, you can break your neck for all I care! He thinks that I'm coining money, or stealing it!"

Fedir slushed through the mud on the way to his house and kept on whispering:

"And where have I spent my strength, Andriyko?[4] Have I lost it by having a good time, or in drinking? Why, it is still with you; it sits right in your own yard. And where have I spent my strength, Andriyko?"

When he got inside, he took off his old battered boots and lay down on the bed. He lay there till the evening, and fell asleep without having his supper. The roosters had not yet begun to crow when he sprang up and struck his hips against the boards. Again he lay down and again he sprang up. An autumn night was looking at him through a small window. Perhaps it was not the night but murky grief that wailed in the corners of his house and stared at him with its greyish merciless eye. It stiffened him so hard that he could not stir, and showed him something that appeared like images on the window, like visions in the air. . . .

There he is sitting among little Jews, looking after them, tending them, while they are pulling him by the hair and spitting in his face.

Or again, he is kneeling in the church, in that corner where the beggars knock their foreheads against the floor.[5] He is knocking his even louder than the others; and then he sees all the women there come up to him and each give him a loaf of bread. He puts the loaves inside the front part of his shirt, and, as he puts them there, he becomes so broad that the people have to make

4 Diminutive of Andriy, Andrew.
5 Deep genuflections.

way for him. And he feels such shame, such shame as makes his forehead throb with pain.

There he is now, walking across the garden toward Kurochka's house. He is not walking but stealing up to the barn. He pulls a small sheaf of straw from the roof, spills some embers from his pipe on it and runs as fast as he can. Behind him he senses, as if he saw it with his own eyes, that from under the thatched roof there darts out a slender red tonguelet; it darts out and hides itself again and again. . . .

"O-o-oh! Ah-h-h!"

That tonguelet seared his very brain. By means of all the strength in him he freed himself from those unseen trammels, sprang to his feet and looked at the small window. Like an executioner, it pierced him through and through. He knew that it would again knock him down and torture him with its visions, and he became frightened, because he saw no way out for himself. Suddenly he turned on the spot and looked for a place through which he might escape. Before him he saw some kind of a gate open up. He felt relieved and quickly rushed through it.

II

He may have been sixteen years old when he left his village. He never again saw such a bright day, such a joyful sun. It fondled the green grasses, the blue forests and the shiny rivers. He turned to look at the village. If only someone had come and said a kind word to him, he would have returned. How gladly he would have returned!

"He beats me, beats me so terribly, won't give me anything to eat or to wear!"

His voice reverberated as it rolled upon the tall grasses.

"Father, I hope the earth in which you lie will never devour you!"

He walked even faster, passed the village fields, two more villages, and from the top of a hillock saw the town which shone in the sun like a sparkling dragon.

*　*　*

All were amazed at his strength, and feared him. The Jews did not shove him around and the labourers did not make fun of him or abuse him with their pranks. He hurled heavy sacks as if they were stuffed dumplings from the dray into the granary and out of the granary into the dray. Day in and day out.

"My back is cracking from those heavy sacks."

"Drink whiskey, it'll get numb."

And really, his back would get numb from the whiskey, as if with a wave of the hand.

And on Sundays and holy days, together with his friends, he would go to a tavern. These taverns stood beyond the town, actually between the town and the village. The ones who had no work in the village would first go there, and those who had nothing to do in the town would show up there too. They all liked it, for it was neither a village nor a town.

What amusements they had in those taverns!

At first the gentry from the town took the lead. They spoke of their former affluence, how much money they received from the Emperor's[6] treasury on the first of the month, what expensive clothes they wore. The muzhiks[7] listened and, out of great respect for them, treated them to whiskey. But when they themselves got somewhat drunk, they broke out of the townsmen's domination, and then the gentry were hard put to it.

"Come now, lords,[8] let's get more lively. Clutch each other around the necks and dance a polka for us, so that we can see what life is like among such great nobles."

The gentry danced. They had to. The muzhiks encircled them and guffawed so loud that the tavern trembled.

"Up, down, up, down! Hop! Skip!"

"Once more."

"Easy now, all together glide along!"

"Stop, it's enough! Now drink your whiskey, pick up your noble lice, put them in your pockets, and get out of the tavern, because the muzhiks want to dance and have some fun by themselves."

And the gentry slipped out like timid rabbits.

"I can handle those town folks alright! The whole lot of them are as light as feathers; all you have to do is blow on them and off they fly."

6 Austrian.
7 Common peasants.
8 Spoken sarcastically of the gentry.

"Hey, Yudko,[9] let's have some whiskey, give us beer, rum. You know what's what."

The Jew quickly put everything they asked for and took the money from them as soon as he served them.

"Listen, you Bezklubiy,[10] what are you bawling about? Because you are hipless? Drink and shut your big trap, because I want to have some fun."

Bezklubiy bawled even louder.

"Quiet, or I'll let you have one!"

"Don't touch him."

"And who are you?"

"Who do you think you are, a lord?"

Fedir arose from behind the table and smacked the challenger in the face.

"So you're thrashing[11] on Sunday? Why, it's a sin!"

With a blow he knocked Fedir down to the floor. Two groups formed. Everything in the tavern went topsy-turvy. The Jew ran away, the whiskey spilled down to the floor, the tables and benches reddened with blood, broke and fell down in pieces. The two groups lay and groaned in the slime of their spittle, whiskey and blood. Bezklubiy sat alone in the corner and bellowed like an ox. No one knew why.

In a while policemen came rushing in and began to sober up the poor wretches. With brute force they were hauled to their feet again and again and each time knocked down with a single blow. The poor devils crashed to the floor like sturdy oaks and raised themselves up like wet clay. When the police finally managed to sober them up, they took them to prison.

* * *

He drove down the road between the fields on a dray full of sacks. The wheat and rye appeared like golden and silver groves, and under the slight breeze the spikes swayed toward one another. Above that gold and silver there floated light dark cloudlets like a thin silken net. There was a sea of sunlight in the sea of endless grainfields. Under the spikes the earth sounded shrilly, sang out, and seemed to express itself in words.

[9] A Jewish name.
[10] Surname, meaning Hipless.
[11] Beating, fighting.

"Moshko,[12] rein in the horses, because I'm going away."

He leaped down from the dray and went along the boundary lines and across the fields. Before evening he reached Andriy Kurochka's estate.

"You must be either a thief or a scoundrel, because a good man doesn't leave his village to go roaming far and wide."

"You'll see for yourself. Whatever my father didn't squander away in drinking, he sold during the hungry years. Then he took in my sister's husband and shortly after he died. His son-in-law beat me as long as I could stand it, and then I ran away."

"I hear that the Boykos[13] still plow with cows, is that true?"

"No, the Germans, it seems, are in the neighborhood, and they plow with cows."

"Pull off your pighide shoes[14] and take your sheepskin coat outside, so that you don't leave any vermin around here. Then lie down and sleep. By the way, is there a church in your district, such as ours? Is there a priest?"

"The same as here."

"Well, I'll see how you make out. If you're not eager to steal and aren't afraid of work, maybe I'll hire you."

He was hired. The villagers found that he was not a thief but a good worker, and that he was doing his best to better his lot. For that reason they accepted him as one of their own. He became familiar with the different fields, knew to whom they belonged, which was becoming swampy and which was drying out, who was the worst thief and who was the most wealthy. In the end he became a real villager.

After he had served for several years, certain well-meaning people began to advise him to become a landed man himself. One of them said:

"Don't be a fool. If you get a plot of garden as a dowry, and the wench is strong and well provided for, take her. And if you've saved some of the money you've been earning, and earn a little more, go ahead and build yourself a house. Even if it does look like a coop, still it will be yours. Then, if it rains or is wintertime, or if there's no work for a while, you won't have to whimper and

---

12 Colloquial for Moses.
13 Ukrainians living in Western Ukraine, in the Carpathian region of Striy and Sambir.
14 Similar to moccasins.

shiver behind the rich man's corner, or rot in the mangers, because you'll have a nook of your own. Listen to an old man who knows what he's talking about."

* * *

He married, started to build a house, and worked so hard for himself and for others that he almost cracked from the exertion. On his own back he hauled the boards from the town, worked for old sheaves of straw which he took to thatch his roof, earned money to pay first for the windows, then for the doors. Two years passed before he finished building his cottage. It was a small, insignificant looking hut. Among the other cottages it appeared like a scraggy chicken let in among a flock of splendid birds. But such as it was, Fedir was pleased with it.

* * *

About fifteen years went by. Then, one day the church banners were brought in front of Fedir's home. Inside, on a bench lay his Katerina – so huge and swollen that she was a frightful sight. Beside him Fedir held his two daughters: eleven-year-old Nastia[15] and Mariyka[16] who was eight. And he kept on asking them: "My daughters, what are we going to do without our mother? Which one of you will cook meals for your daddy?"

And when they were about to place his wife in the coffin, he raised a lament.

"Lift her easy, because her body is racked with pain. O, my dear Katerina, I haven't had time even to talk with you as much as I would have liked. That's why you became angry and left me."

He fell upon the deceased woman and began kissing her face.

"People, good people, I've never spoken a word to her and, as I worked endlessly, I had forgotten she was alive and never thought of talking with her. Forgive me, dear Katerina, my good friend."

The women's wailing rushed out of the house and sped far into the village.

"Friends, when she married me, it was as though she dove into the water never to appear again. Nobody ever saw her among people. It's only now that she emerged among you, there on the bench. I never spoke to her a single word, not even a paltry one. . . ."

[15] Colloquial for Anasthasia.
[16] Diminutive of Mary.

Several more years passed. One evening Nastia came from the place where she worked to visit him. Fedir glanced at her and grew pale.

"Nastia, my poor girl! Have you come alone? Where's your husband?"

Nastia began to sob and wail, but he did not say another word to her. Only when he took her back to the town where she worked and was parting with her did he speak:

"My dear child, may God treat you the best He can. But see that you don't do away with the child, because you'll never be able to cover your shame, and if you commit such a sin, you'll never be pardoned. Send me news how it will be with you here."

* * *

More years passed. Time did not stand still. Fedir did not let go of the flail all winter, held on to the plow all spring, and to the scythe all summer. His bones ached; their joints rubbed off and burned him. Sunday, however, came to his help, because on Sunday he could go to his cherry tree and lie down under it on the green grass which sucked out his pain into the earth. But the time came when even Sunday could not improve that which the weekdays damaged, and the grass could not draw out the pain which had hardened in his old bones. In addition, a harsh cough had settled in him and would not leave him, no matter what he was doing – mowing, plowing or flailing.

* * *

It was beginning to dawn. The small window was already white when Fedir returned from the long journey through his past life. He washed himself, said his prayers and began getting ready to go to the landlord's manor.

"I'll hire myself out to the landlord from the beginning of spring. In the meantime I'll get some money from him in advance for boots and some food to tide me over the winter somehow, and then I'll start working for him."

III

White narrow pathways throughout the village linked all the cottages together. Only Fedir's cottage stood abandoned beyond that network of paths. Fedir hibernated like a bear. In the morning he got up for an hour or so to make fire and cook himself a meal, and then passed the rest of the day and all night lying on top of the clay-stove. The farther the winter advanced, the more did his mind become childish.

"Now, Fedir, my dear fellow, get up and cut yourself a slice of bread, but a thin one, just like the rich people do, because I feel that you've become hungry."

He laughed, climbed down from the stove, cut the bread, held the slice up to the window to see if it was thin, like that of the rich people.

And during the dark winter nights, his loud voice filling the entire hut, he spoke of terrible things.

"The village had died off completely, and I don't even think of it. I don't even look that way."

But his words pervaded him with fright. Covered with sweat from fear, he leaped down from the stove and rushed to the small window to convince himself that there was light in the tavern. Relieved, he returned to the top of the stove.

And when he awoke from sleep during the night, he could not regain his senses or remember who he was. Only when he banged his fists against the beam in the ceiling did he come to.

That winter his hut was invaded by vampires, phantoms and spectres. They bustled about the room like mischievous children. They flew into the porch[17] and made the house chilly. They ran up the stove flues into the attic and knocked about so hard that the ceiling cracked. Rapping on the windows, they tried to lure him outside. He would not give in to them, tried not to be frightened, but they clambered up to the top of the stove, pinched him, choked him, stuffed his mouth with foot-clouts. One night all the devils flew into the hut. They danced and stamped so loudly that the entire house shook, and raised such a cold wind that he felt as if he were freezing to death. Then they all sat around the table and, out of exhaustion, let their tongues hang from their mouths; and their tongues were similar to the one he had placed under Kurochka's barn. He lay there like one dead, and only when the roosters began to crow did he raise himself with an effort and began to say his prayers. But even as he tried saying them, the fiends did not give him any peace. He could not remember those prayers which he knew best, and even forgot how to cross himself. Those phantoms harassed him so much that when spring arrived he could hardly breathe and became as white as paper.

17 Usually a hallway covered on all sides.

"I must get the money somehow and call the priest to bless the house, because all the impure things from the whole village have crawled in here on top of one another. They've drained so much of my blood that the wind just knocks me off my feet."

When the spring shone forth, he rubbed his old boots with grease, patched his shirts, twined ties for his pighide shoes and rejoiced at the thought that finally he would go to serve at the manor.

"I'll dress myself nicely, pull on my boots, and off to the mansion yard. I'll say: 'May it please your lordship, I'm reporting for work on your estate.' "

"Good, Fedir," he imagined the landlord saying to him. "As I can see, you're the right kind of man if you report according to the regulation."

And as he was patching his shirt, Fedir smiled sweetly.

* * *

Fedir stood in the middle of the landlord's barnyard and looked sadly at a file of plows passing through the gate. The file was like a chain in which the iron seemed to merge the men's flesh with that of the oxen.

"My plowing is over. The old worn-out link had to be cast away, otherwise the chain might snap in the middle of the road."

He shook his head and went to the barn to get some grain for the swine. In the barnyard it was quiet all day. Only the shouting of the women and the crying of the children reached him from the servants' hovels.

If anyone picked out the worst huts in the village and drove into them the most ragged muzhiks and women with faces all yellow, and to all that added some naked small fry, the children, and put the whole lot of them into a pile, he would have a true picture of those hovels together with their inhabitants.

From the barnyard Fedir looked at those hovels and gestured with his head, as if he were objecting to something.

"How could one expect me to go there, into such a hell? I'll sleep in the stable now that winter is gone. I won't go into that bottomless pit."

In the evening he went to the stable. Along the mangers stood two long rows of oxen which were lazily chewing the hay. Beside every four of them stood the drivers watching, so that the oxen would not drop any hay under themselves. On the ground between those rows sat the plowmen and sowers. They were patching their pighide shoes, sewing up their torn homespun outer jackets with string, and repairing the plow-scrapers. Everybody was puttering over something or other. They were joined by Fedir. One after another the oxen dropped down on the straw. Their drivers then rolled themselves into the mangers and were soon followed by the plowers. In the stable there began to reign a heavy repose which, after the exhaustive labour in the plowed fields, usually falls upon the workers in it like a heavy boulder. Fedir also pushed himself among the oxen.

"Swineherd, get out from among the oxen and go to your pigs. Would you like us to make a bed for you yet? Your Mariyka is certainly treating us badly. She's in heat, like a bitch, and goes around with the wagoner, giving him the best she has. And yet you come creeping here to bother us. Get away from the oxen."

Fedir crawled out from the manger and lay down by the gate on a scattered bundle of straw. The forgotten injury he had once suffered awakened in him that very instant.

"You have a sin for treating me like that, Andriy, a big sin."

The stable groaned, yawned, and spoke in its sleep. It breathed as hard as if somewhere deep down in the earth thousands of people were being stifled to death.

"Pray for me that God may preserve my reason and prevent me from roasting you in the fire like a porkling, because then it will take you three days at least to scrape up the ashes of all your wealth."

Towards early morning he rolled into the dark abyss of the rustic sleep of the stable.

V

After that Fedir never went to the stable and never talked with the hired hands. He slept in the barn and did not show himself to anyone. After Easter Maria married the wagoner and left to work for another landlord. Fedir followed them as they passed through the gate and, beyond it, said goodbye to them.

"Maria, just remember that in the presence of witnesses I'll hand over the house to Nastia. See that you don't chase her out, because the poor girl is now all alone."

He turned back and went to the pigsty. There, where no one could see him, he started to cry.

"Now live with anybody you like."

That day he got drunk, and in the evening came back to the stable.

"Hey you, wards of the rich, don't chase me out now, because my Mariyka has wandered off."

"Who wants to chase you away? Just lie down and sleep now that your head is so heavy."

"Sure, a drunken man likes to get a good sleep, just as God would like him to. But you're telling me to go to sleep. And now I'm asking you where I'm to go to sleep? If you're such a wise one, tell me, where am I to go to sleep?"

He touched Protz's[18] nose with his, so closely did he approach him with his question.

"Wherever you fall, there you'll sleep."

"And what if I tried the manger, ha?"

He smiled slyly.

"I'll get into the manger and you'll grab me by the shock of my hair, bang me in the neck and chase me out with a cudgel. 'Get out of here, you old cur!' That's what you'll say."

The drivers arose from their mangers to look at the comedy.

"You'll knock me out of the manger, because you were rotting here and must rot away in it, because you don't know what a human being is – you're an ox. You've never seen the inside of a house. And yet you drive a decent man out of the manger with a cudgel! But you ask me: 'And where have you been all this time, my fine fellow?' I'll tell you where: I've been among honest people, and among them I felt good. But you say: 'Why, then, have they chased you away from themselves?' Here's where the knot is. As for the reason, I can't tell you much, just a few words: There is no God among men. But you're supposed to be the wise one. You should know everything."

"Go and sleep it off, old man. Don't talk nonsense. Tomorrow we'll have to go to the village for an election, and there we'll knead those rich fellows a little."

"Sure I'll go to the election, and there I'll tell the people all the wrongs I've suffered. But I won't go into the manger, because I'm not going to rot away there. I know better than you how things should be; I saw more of the world than your master. But wait, I'll tell you everything, as at a court investigation: I carried slops for the Jews, I grovelled under their benches, and lay in prison dirt many times. Let God write down my sins in His book, I'm not afraid. I'll answer for everything, and will tell Him off

[18] Colloquial for Procopius.

just as I would anybody else. And who do you think taught me to stand up for myself? Whatever they could lay their hands on, they beat me with it. Don't worry, I'll tell everything, and I'll get myself out of it. You see, God put into my head sense enough to make me turn to my own kind. When I saw His heavenly grace out in the fields and noticed how the rye begged to be mowed, and heard the peeping cry of the earth: 'Come, Fedir, take the bread off me,' I immediately left the Jew in the middle of the road and went to do God's work. To this day I thank the Lord for that."

He crossed himself, kissed the ground and made deep reverent bows.

"I found myself among my own people, and it seemed that the world had opened up to me. And with them I worked so hard! I got married, and with these calloused hands I built myself a house. Then I expected things to be all right with me. But one must do penance for one's sins. God does not beat you with a rod and have done with it. My Katerina died. Well, that was that. It's His will. It's His command. I enjoyed my children, fed them well, attended to their least needs. Finally, I brought them up, and the people went and made waste of it all. My Nastia is neither here nor there, and went to serve the Jews again, while Maria – look what happened: she wandered off with a Pole. She'll suffer for it. But that's all right. Let God punish me if I say something wrong. Punishment there must be!"

With the tips of his fingers he seized his lips and pressed them tightly together, so as not to say anything that might offend God.

"And I remained almost barefooted! So I went to him[19] in very slushy weather and said to him: 'Give me some money so that I could put something decent on my feet.' And he told me: 'Go to the Jews.' Then I came to you, and you said: 'Get out!' And where am I to go now? God punishes, people punish, you punish. And I just can't stand so much punishment!"

"Go and lie down in the manger, old man. We're asking you to. Go."

"Let the punishment fall on me. I'm ready for it. But let it be just! Tell me, would you like me to eat out all the soft part of the bread and leave you only the burnt crust? You wouldn't like it, would you? It wouldn't be right!"

He tore the front of his shirt, took it off and threw it under the oxen.

[19] Andriy Kurochka.

"Now look at what a crust my rich masters have left for me. What's there left to live with? What's there left to punish?"

Naked, he tumbled to the ground. The hired hands covered him with the best sheets they had.

VI

Two groups stood near the municipal office. One was in rags, apathetic, seemingly alien to the village; the other – clean, well-washed, eager. They were the labourers and their masters. From one and the other group, as their names were called out, individuals entered the office and voted. The steward grew hoarse, because to each worker he had to call out the names of the candidates – the rich one, the reeve and the Jew. The gendarmes moved about and smiled, as if they were enjoying a kind of child's play.

"Well, boys, now that you've elected the landlord, sit down and you'll get some whiskey," said the steward.

The landed men raised their voices.

"What lousy wretches! What beggars! To the landlord they're just cattle."

"Listen, just listen. Do you hear the rich bawling?"

"Let them bawl, as long as we have whiskey to drink."

"Drink brimstone, drink your own blood, you scoundrels!"

"We prefer whiskey."

"It looks like the landlords have found some justification for that hungry rabble to go and make havoc in the village. That's what they've done to us!"

"You, you who have read so much, do you think I haven't been in the Reading Room?[20] Even there the poor stand at the door. Around the table sit the priest, the elders of the church, the rich ones, while the precentor is reading those newspapers. And all you do is keep nodding your heads like oxen, as if you understood anything of it. One and all of you are such fools that you just don't know what's what. And is that what the Reading Room should be? For the rich to sit at the table and for the hired hands to stand at the door? It's the same in church, in the office, everywhere. And do you expect us to stick with you?"

"The common peasant's head is not for reading or writing, and his bottom is not for the chair."

The hirelings burst out laughing.

20 A society where illiterate peasants had newspapers and books read to them.

"Quiet, you grimy ones! Delouse yourselves first and then teach the well-to-do what's what."

"Hey you, Kurochka, are you standing up for the wealthy peasants now too? Why, you're worse than an infidel! What are you hollering for? Just you wait, your wealth will all go to seed. Do you remember the time I laboured for you and got sick from overwork? And did you during all that week bring me a small chunk of bread or a drink of water? Is that how you stand up for the people? I've left all my strength with you, and you chased me out barefoot into the winter cold. Why, you're worse than an infidel, because we don't reckon he belongs to our faith. Just wait and you'll see how your children will squander all your wealth so that not a trace of it will remain. You're a Calvin!"[21]

Kurochka smacked Fedir in the face so hard that blood covered it, and he fell to the ground.

"Boys, come, let's soften up the rich guy a bit."

The hired hands seized Kurochka, but his rich friends came to his defence, and blood began to flow. . . .

VII

Fedir lay in bed in his house. His eyes burned like glowing coals. They were enkindled by those red tonguelets which in thousands of tiny flames coursed through his body and scorched him, reducing him to cinders. Those tonguelets flashed like lightning in all his veins and returned to his eyes. He gnawed his fists, and banged his forehead against the wall to make the fire drop out of his eyes.

He seemed all aflame and felt the fire blazing out of him. He pressed his eyes hard with both his hands. A horrible outcry, a superhuman scream was heard. The tonguelets flew out of his body and became stuck to the small window panes. He sprang up. The window reddened like a fresh wound and poured blood into the hut.

"Let everything that's mine burn out. All that I've left in his yard."

He leaped about, danced, guffawed. . . .

The small window trembled, shuddered, and let more blood fill the hovel.

He made a dash and stopped on the doorstep.

Embers of wood and flaming straw were falling down to earth

[21] It was an extreme insult for a Ukrainian Greek Catholic to be called a Calvin.

like stars, the forest stood as rigid as rock, and enraged voices broke somewhere out of the ground and immediately were lost. The houses revived, trembled, and were roasting in the fire.

"I don't want what belongs to others. Only what's mine, let that burn out."

C. H. A.

Maple Leaves

The godparents were seated at the table, on the front and rear benches. Nearby stood the bed covered with a sheet. The children, sitting on the edge of the clay-stove,[1] let down their sleeves and looked like a bevy of quails resting, but ever ready to fly. On the other hand, the godparents sat as if they were rooted to the ground, only their hands reaching for the bread or the glasses of whiskey, though they would have preferred that even their hands had remained motionless, bent tightly into a fist and resting on their knees. They picked up the bread and whiskey listlessly. The oil lamp flickered on the top of the oven, forming the godparents into large black shadows which it cast onto the ceiling. There, broken across the beams, they likewise maintained their relative immobility.

Leaning forward near the table stood Ivan, the host, and father of the child who had just been baptized.

"Come, my friends, be so good as to have another round of drinks. It's more like muddy swill than whiskey, but that's the way it is with the muzhik: whatever is the worst in the world, that he has to eat, whatever is the hardest in the world to do, that he must carry out...."

"That's what we were born for," the godparents answered piously.

When the glass had gone the round. Ivan laid it on its side beside the bottle, fearing that, being small, it might fall on the floor.

[1] See page 27.

"Come now, have a snack. . . . Just imagine what trouble has come upon me right in the middle of the harvest, in the very heat of the work. By God, I don't know what to make of it; whether to leave harvesting and take care of my wife and cook for the children, or leave them all here to the mercy of God and, though hungry, go and swing my scythe. That's the way it'll have to be, because at a time like this no one will come to the house to help, not even for a lot of money. 'Here's another child for you, Ivan. Go ahead and rejoice, for you haven't enough of them yet!' "

"Don't grumble, crony, and don't insult God, for it's His will, not yours. As for the children, they're like froth on the water. . . . A stroke of fate, and you'll be carrying them all to the grave."

"No such stroke of fate for me. It will strike where there's only one. A poor beggar should not cuddle up to his wife; he shouldn't even glance in her direction. That would be the best for him. Then even God wouldn't give him more."

"Now you're talking nonsense, buddy. It'll never be that way, because human beings must reproduce."

"If only they were human beings, but they're beggars who are multiplying. That's why I say: 'You beggar, stop breeding, stop reproducing like mice, be content that you've a rag on your back, that you have a chunk of bread to keep you from feeling hungry, and that no one is walloping you in the face. When you have these three things, you're really well off. But stay away from your wife."

"Ivan, my chum, calm yourself a little, for the good of your wife. In her condition, she shouldn't be listening to this, for such talk doesn't bring health. Some other, more suitable time, we'll. . . ."

"I apologize very much to you for this kind of talk of mine, but do you think that I care about her, or worry about my children, or about myself? By God, I don't care! Let them be snatched off, and me with them! So what? What paradise would we lose on earth, what fortunes would we leave behind?"

The godparents said nothing more, nor did they contradict him, for they knew that they could not convince Ivan. They only wished that he would soon talk himself out and let them go home to sleep. Ivan got up from the table, paused in the middle of the room, letting his shirt sleeves down, just like his children on top of the clay-stove, and began to speak to the little ones:

"Well, why don't you fly away from my worried head? I'll even open the windows and doors for you, and off with you!"

The children crept farther away on the stove until they were out of sight.

"What a plague of locusts! All they want is bread, bread. But where am I going to get that bread for them? For that twelfth sheaf one has to make many a sweep with the scythe, and bend down quite a number of times, while pain racks your back and spills over into your shirt-front like glowing coals. Every single stem stabs you in the heart."

This was for the children. Now he turned to the godparents.

"And in the evening, no sooner do you show yourself in the cottage, feeling like a straw insole or a wash-rag, all worn out, then in a single voice the wife and the children greet you: 'There's no bread!' And you, poor fellow, don't go to sleep, but drag the flail and thresh out there in the dark so that tomorrow they will have something to put through the hand-mill. And the flail just shoves you down onto the sheaf and you lie there stiffened until morning comes and you're all covered with the dew. As soon as you peel open your eyes, the dew is already nipping you, as though misery has not nipped you enough. It finds you even during the night. Then you rinse your eyes and drag yourself to the field, feeling as dark and gloomy as if the sun was dimming right in front of you."

"Ivan, don't worry about your children, because not only you but God also is their father, and much older than you."

"I'm not trying to grip God by the shoulders, but why does He let them loose into the world, naked among thorns? He just dumps them on earth without giving them a chance to earn a proper livelihood, sends them no manna from the sky, and then the whole world screams: 'Muzhiks are thieves, robbers, murderers!' One after another they lean on the church pulpit, looking so sleek that a fly would slide off them, and all they do is blame and scold. 'You,' they say, 'don't teach your children the fear of God. You yourselves send them to steal'. . . . Bah, how could I ever chide mine like that? If only there was a maid, a nurse, a governess to look after my children; if only people would supply me with everything, then I, too, would know how to teach them, Reverend Father! But my children grow up in the weeds, among the chickens. And when something happens, as now, then no one knows what they have been eating all day. Whether they steal, whether they beg, or whether they go out to pasture, how am I to know? I mow your fields and forget not only about the children but don't even think about myself. You'd like me to work your fields and teach my children? And what are you for? Yes, my good people, you yourselves know what our life is like."

"We know, buddy, we know. Why shouldn't we know when we ourselves are wading in it?"

"I look at my children, but I don't wonder whether they're well-behaved or know how to do things right. All I want to see is whether they've already learned to walk well enough on the ground so that I can hustle them into some kind of work for others, that's what I wait for. I don't wait until they've gained strength and grown tough, or lived at my side till they're big enough. Just let some rich peasant or squire open his mug, and I fling them right into it, as long as I get rid of them. Then they run about taking care of the cattle, their feet one big sore. The dew stings them, the stubble pricks them, and they just hop around and cry. I myself would help them drive the cattle from the fields where they're not supposed to let them graze, kiss their sore feet, for I have fathered them, and my conscience pricks me painfully, but I avoid them and even hide myself so as not to hear them."

He was flushed and out of breath.

"And so they grow in mangers, under the table or bench, gnaw at their fists, and wash themselves with tears. And when they grow big enough, no doubt they steal, for, never having known abundance, they cheer themselves with pilfered things. You look, and see the gendarme coming to you. He handcuffs you, beats you up as if you were an animal, because you are the father of a thief and must be plotting with him. And then you're branded a thief forever! But that's not all. The end is still ahead. Suppose your son, a child of yours but a thief to others, rots in jail. A thief is not to be pitied. Let him rot! But they take away his health, send him to a hospital, and then write to the reeve that the father should pay the costs. They drive you out of your house and throw you beneath the hedge, guts and all! You go to the reeve and kiss his hands. 'My dear reeve, spare me this punishment.' 'You,' says the reeve, 'you're a poor man, so maybe we'll let you go free. But what favour will I get for my favour?' — You shrug your shoulders, fold yourself like a jack-knife, and say: 'I'll work a whole month for you for nothing'. . . . Is it so or not, good people? Am I telling the truth or am I barking lies, like a dog?"

"It's all true. Everything is just like that. You haven't said a single word that's wrong."

Ivan trembled all over, and felt the full weight of his own terrifying words.

"Let none of you, good people, say that I caw over the heads of my children, like a raven over a carcass, let no one say that, good people, not one of you! I don't caw, I only speak the truth. It's my grief that's cawing; it's my heart that caws!"

His eyes lit up. In them appeared a fierce love for his children, and with his eyes he searched the room for them.

"It looks like I've really wronged my children, much worse than any blackguard enemy would. But I, as you can see, have not wronged them; I've only opened my eyes to see what's happening today, what will be tomorrow, and in the years that will follow one another, to see how my children are doing. And what I've seen, that I've told you. I went to visit them, and my blood just congealed at the sight of their sorry plight on the land. . . ."

After a pause, he added:

"If only there weren't any oceans to that Canada out there! I'd put them all in a sack and take them there on foot so as to carry them far away from this outrage. I'd go around those oceans, trudging along their coasts. . . ."

The godparents had forgotten about their rest, but now, having recalled it, they hastily arose and departed.

II

It was early in the morning.

The children were eating their noonday meal on the floor. They clacked their spoons and used them so clumsily that the food spilled over their shirt fronts. Nearby lay their mother, thin and jaundiced, with her knees doubled below her breasts. Down her black, uncombed tresses flowed pain and torment, while she tightened her lips so as not to cry out. The children, with spoons in their mouths, kept turning around to glance at their mother, and again returned to the bowl.

"Semenko,[2] have you finished eating?"

"Yes," answered the six-year-old boy.

"Then take the whisk-broom, sprinkle the floor and sweep the room. Mother can't bend down because she has a pain inside. Don't raise too much dust."

"Move away, because I can't sweep with you there."

The mother got up and with difficulty staggered to her bed.

[2] Diminutive of Semen, Simeon or Simon.

"Now, Semenko, wash yourself properly, and let Katrusia[3] and Maria wash themselves too. Then take the pitcher and hurry to fetch some water, but don't fall into the well as you're dipping, don't lean over too far. . . ."

"Semenko, go out and pick some cucumbers and put them into the winnowing basket, so that mother can pickle them in the crock, for I can see that I'll be sick for some time yet, and then you wouldn't have anything to eat with the bread. And pick some dill and cherry leaves. But don't break off any vines, just pluck the cucumbers at the stalks. . . ."

"Semenko, gather the shirts off the racks, so that I could patch them up, because you're walking around as black as crows."

* * *

Semenko was constantly on the run, doing whatever his mother asked him to. From time to time he pushed his younger sisters around and said that girls didn't know anything except to eat.

"They're still small, Semenko. When they grow up, they'll wash the shirts for you."

"I'm going to hire myself out somewhere, and there they'll wash the shirts for me. I don't need people like them."

"Don't be so glad about hiring yourself out, for many times you'll spend your days in weeping."

"Look at daddy. He grew up as a hired hand, and there's nothing wrong with him."

"You too will grow up as a hired hand, and you'll work so hard that your skin will crack from labor. But don't talk so much, Semenko. Get ready to take lunch to daddy. He must be so hungry by now that he has strained his eyes looking for you."

"I must take daddy's cane to drive the dogs away."

"What if you should lose it? Then daddy will beat us both. Don't go bareheaded. At least take daddy's hat."

"The hat will only fall over my eyes and I won't see the road."

"Wash the pitcher and fill it up with borshch."[4]

"You don't have to tell me so much. I know what to do."

"Semenko, see that the dogs don't bite you."

III

He hurried with short steps through the thick layer of dust, and left small footprints behind him that seemed like white flowers.

3 Diminutive of Katerina, Catherine.
4 Beet soup.

"Gosh, before I get there the sun will roast me, but good! I'll have to fix my hair like a soldier, and then it'll be more comfortable for me to walk."

He put the lunch down on the road and piled his hair on top of his head in order to press it down with the hat and look like a soldier with a crewcut. His eyes smiling, he jumped up quickly and toddled ahead. But soon his hair slipped from under the wide hat and covered his neck.

"This is a stupid hat. Just wait till I hire myself out. Then I'll have such a hat that. . . ."

He licked his lips in anticipation. Having covered some distance along the road, he again set the lunch on the ground.

"I'm going to draw me a large wheel with spokes."

He sat down in the middle of the road, in the dust, circled the cane around himself and then went tracing the beams of the wheel. He got up abruptly, jumped over the crooked circle and ran, feeling very happy.

He approached each gate stealthily, peered in to see if there was a dog in the yard, and only when he did not see any would he run past. From one yard a dog rushed out and pursued him. Semenko screeched and screamed, and, holding on to the lunch, sat down on the ground. The cane fell on the road. He sat huddled for a long time, waiting for the dog to bite him. After a while he dared to look up, and saw a black dog standing quietly beside him.

"Here, Gypsy, here, have some cornmeal, but don't bite me, because it hurts so much, and your master would have to pay a fine. He'd break your legs if he had to pay that fine for you."

He pinched off pieces from the chunk of cornmeal wrapped in a cloth and tossed it bit by bit to the dog. He laughed at the way the animal caught them in the air. The dog had his mouth open, and so did the boy.

"Who are you, imp? Feeding dogs on the road? And what'll you have left to take to the fields?"

Some woman had come upon him and whacked him on the back of the neck.

"Just what I need – to be hit when the dog was about to tear me to pieces!"

"Whose boy are you? And such a polite one!"

"I'm Ivan Petriv's boy. Mother has just had a baby and is sick, and I have to carry the lunch. Dogs bite me, and yet you have to come along and beat me!"

"Oh, I haven't beaten you that hard. . . . Where are you taking the lunch?"

"I'm taking it to daddy, to the landlord's field by the pond."

"Come along with me, you nuisance, for I'm taking a lunch there too."

They walked together.

"And who prepared the lunch?"

"Mother cooked it, because I don't know how to do it yet, and Maria and Katerina are smaller than me."

"But isn't your mother sick?"

"Sure she's sick. She rolls on the ground and groans something awful. But I do the work for her."

"My, what a worker!"

"You don't know how it is, and that's why you talk so silly. Just ask my mother how smart I am. I know the whole Lord's Prayer."

The woman laughed, and Semenko shrugged his shoulders and became silent.

The dog ran after him, and the boy pretended to be throwing pieces of cornmeal to him, thus luring the dog to follow him.

IV

It was three days later.

Semenko and his sisters sat in the middle of the room. The trough with the little baby in it also stood there. Beside them there was a dishful of green sliced cucumbers and bread. Their mother was lying on the bed. She was surrounded by green willow branches.[5] Above her buzzed a swarm of flies.

"Finish eating and sit quietly, because I'm going to take the baby over to Vasyl's[6] wife so she can nurse it. Daddy said to take it there in the morning, at noon and towards the evening. In the evening he will take it there himself."

"Semenko, don't break the baby in two."

"I thought you were asleep. Daddy said I should give you cold water, and a bun to eat. Maria is so nice that she grabbed the bun and took one bite out of it. But I spanked her and took it away. Are you going to eat it?"

5 This is a custom when a person is about to die.
6 Basil.

"No, I don't want it."

"Daddy also twisted and made a candle and said that, if you were dying, I was to light it and put it in your hands. But I don't know when I should give it to you."

The mother looked at her son with large, shining eyes. Her unfathomable sadness, immense grief, and helpless fear combined to produce two large pearl-like tears in her eyes. They rolled slowly onto her eyelids and congealed upon them.

"Daddy also cried in the porch this morning. Oh, how he banged his head against the doorpost! Still in tears, he took the scythe and left."

The boy picked up the baby and went out.

* * *

"Semenko, see that you don't let a step-mother spank Katrusia and Mariyka and Vasylko.[7] Do you hear? Because a step-mother will beat you, drive you away from food, and not give you white shirts to wear."

"I won't let her, and I'll tell daddy."

"Nothing will help, my dearest son, my most precious child. And when you all grow up, see that you love one another very, very much. You'll have to help them. Don't let anybody do them any harm."

"When I grow up strong and get a job, I'll take care of them. I'll come to see them every Sunday."

"Semenko, tell daddy that mother begged him to love you all...."

"Mother, eat this bun."

"Sing to the baby, so it doesn't cry."

Semenko rocked the baby, but did not know how to sing. Then the mother wiped her dry lips with the palm of her hand and began to sing.

In a weak, halting voice her soul flowed out of her, descending very softly among the children, tenderly kissing them on their heads. Her soft, indistinct words were saying that the wind had strewn tiny maple leaves over the barren fields, and no one could gather them, nor would they ever be green again. The song endeavoured to get out of the house and fly into the empty fields to follow those tiny leaves.

7 Diminutive of Vasyl, Basil.

The Dream

He was sound asleep.

The forest groaned and murmured, as slight whispers[1] tore themselves away from the thin branches and fell down to earth with chilly hoar-frost on them. Like so many diminutive bells did they fall.

The wind howled like a dog in pursuit.

The sky was clear and hard as oak, and the moon in it appeared as bright as on Christmas Eve.

The third-share[2] cropper was fast asleep. He rested his head on his own pile of corn, and his feet on the two belonging to the landlord. His black hair was grey from hoar-frost and his jacket, turned rusty in color, had become white. His sturdy hands did not feel cold, and his wind-burned face seemed like a brick.

He talked in his sleep, emitting from his lips a sheaf of white breath after every word. His voice followed the wind to the forest where for a long time it beat about from tree to tree.

"Don't you dare touch it, because it has been honestly earned. And you're taking it away. . . . What a wealthy man you've found in me!"

He raised his fist, but it fell feebly on the dry cornstalks.

"I'm able to work, my hands are as hard as horses' hoofs. I'll clout you once and knock the life out of you!

"Kiss the soil wherever you happen to walk, because it feeds you and makes things grow, whether it belongs to you or not. It's true, yes, it certainly is! Land is the means to everything – if it's yours. It will warm you, cover you, nourish you, and make others respect you."

His sudden coughing was like the sound of big horns blowing.

"If you haven't your own tilled land, you haven't a place to set your foot on; no place at all; nothing, simply nothing. . . ."

He put his fist under his head.

"I've toiled hard on other people's fields. But God gave me my chance. May He do the same to everyone else. He took and gave it to me. 'Here you are,' He said, 'a small piece of land for you. But keep it, don't let it go. Hang on to it with your very teeth, and love it as you would a wife who is much to your liking.' "

---

[1] Poetic for the sound of falling leaves as they detach themselves from the branches.

[2] One who works for every third part of what he does in the field.

His hat fell off his head and rolled away in the wind.

"Hey, Tanasko,[3] take off your hat. This is the first time you've come into the fields this spring – it's the proper thing to do. God willing, there will be wheat. We will bake loaves of plaited bread and give them to those who haven't any flour to bake with. We'll give, we'll give, – as God has given to us. We'll give to others, we will."

He was now lying crosswise.

"The boundary line is also eager to produce blades of grain, because the boundary is also soil, it's more than that. I'll leave it to you when I die. See, it's as flat as a tablecloth, only it's black. I'll cover your table in the field with this cloth, and you will eat and thank God you had such a father.

"The spring is lovely. Go ahead and plow the land, but don't leave any strips unplowed. Water the oxen and return home before sundown, because to neglect the cattle is a greater sin than...."

He awoke and caught the sound of the last few words he uttered in his dream. He looked up at the sky and searched for the Hen.[4] Then he passed his hand across his bare chest and crossed himself.

"Such fierce cold just at the beginning of autumn! Before you know it, the snow will cover everything. It'll soon be winter, and here I was dreaming of such a beautiful spring.... Alright, Yakiv,[5] go on husking corn. You've slept long enough!"

The Basarabs

Toma[1] Basarab wanted to hang himself in the granary precisely at noontime. But his wife screamed so loud that all the men in

---

[3] Colloquial for Athanasius.

[4] The Hen and its six chicks. The name which the peasants apply to the cluster of stars, the Pleiades, in the constellation Taurus. By the position of the Hen, they can tell the time at night.

[5] Jacob, James.

[1] Thomas.

the neighborhood dropped their flails, all the women came rushing out of the porches, and dashed into Toma's yard. Brave Antin,[2] the one who pulled teeth at ten kreutzers each, climbed into the granary, and only God knows how he managed it, but he did drag out Toma who was still breathing. In the meantime the entire yard became filled with adults and children. They stood and looked on with great fear.

"Well, why do you stand there as if it were the eve of a wedding? Help me get him into the house. What a brainless mob! Do you think he's going to bite you?"

They carried Toma into the house, and the crowd departed through the gate and began to pass judgment, everyone in his own particular manner.

"The Basarabs are again starting to hang themselves. They're not well in the head."

"It's only three years ago that Les[3] tried to string himself up. Lord! What a storm arose at that time. It tore the whole gable-end off my house."

"The Basarabs must have something wrong in them if they keep on destroying themselves one after another."

"I remember the time when Nikolay Basarab hanged himself; after him Ivan Basarab committed suicide the same way, and before the year was over, one early morning Vasyl[4] suspended himself from a small cherry tree. He shook all its blossoms and his hair was full of those white blooms. That's three already, and I consider myself still a young man – I may or may not yet be thirty-five years old."

"That's what you remember, but I recall the time when their great-grandfather dangled from a joist. He was extremely rich, kept his money dry on a bedthrow and never went anywhere on foot. He had such a jet-black horse that used to jump over the gate, and he always held the knout handy. It was said that, under serfdom, he would drive people to work for him with that knout, tearing off their flesh with it. And then one morning the news spread that the old master was hanging from a joist. I was still a child then, but, as if it were today, I see a crowd of people in his yard. When they cut him loose and were carrying him toward the porch, he looked so terrible that the women wailed from

2 Anthony.
3 Colloquial for Oles, Alexander.
4 Basil.

fright. The men didn't care, and simply said: 'Ah, now you won't lift off our skins in chunks, because the fiend has already raised you up to a joist.' After that, in a day or two, such a storm sprang up, such a wind blew that it tore out trees by the roots and lifted roofs off houses."

"People still point out the Basarab graves in the old cemetery behind the mound. They are buried in unconsecrated ground and not in the graveyard itself. Those are the graves beyond the old cemetery and the new one, and the Basarabs are the only ones buried there."

"And do you think that the priest has the right to bury such a one in the cemetery? Even if someone were to give him all his property, it wouldn't be permitted. How could such an accursed person be shoved among decent people?"

"Oh, yes, the Basarabs will now lower their heads. They'll walk about wretched and unhappy."

"Only if this one doesn't drag others after him, because the same evil thing persecutes them all. Just look, one has committed suicide, and, as you continue to look, ten others are ready to go the same way. They're all tied together. Calamity leads them all on the same string."

"It will continue strangling them in the same manner till the seventh generation. And when the seventh generation passes away, it will have no more power over them. Some one of them surely earned the wrath of God. Indeed, cronies, that's quite a punishment – to inflict such a penalty through the seventh lifetime of flesh and bone. God hasn't any worse punishment on earth."

"In their case, it's clear that God is punishing them. He gives them wealth; He gives them brains; they are all prosperous. And then, all of a sudden, He takes it all away from them and hoists them up to a beam."

"One only needs to look at their eyes. They are not eyes but dark wounds in the forehead which live and rot. One of them has eyes like bottomless pits; they look but see nothing, because they aren't meant for seeing. In another, only one of the eyes is alive, and all around it the rest is stone – the forehead is stone, the face is stone, everything. And this Toma, did he ever look at a man the way one ought to? His eyes seemed to be turned on you, but they looked somewhere into himself, into his abysmal depths."

"Their eyes are looking into that ancient sin for which they are punished. The sin had been placed inside them, so that they all might see it and have no peace, so that the punishment might go on."

"The Basarabs are born, grow wealthy, and lose their souls, so that other people might repent."

"They have a heavy burden of sin in their family and must carry it to the end, even if all of them go to seed."

"Sin, comrades, sin does not pass us by. One must be redeemed from it. It will pass on to the child, take hold of the cattle, set stacks on fire, fall as hail on the green fields, and will grasp a man's soul and turn it over to eternal suffering."

The women listened fearfully and all but crossed themselves, the children sat among them, and the men continued to discuss sin for a long time until finally they sauntered off to the tavern.

II

The Basarabs were all gathered at the home of Semen[5] Basarab's widow,[6] because she was the oldest and wealthiest of their clan. They also brought Toma along. Semen's widow prepared plenty of food, provided all kinds of drinks, and seated her relatives around the large table, placing Toma in the seat of honor.

"Todoska,[7] don't weep, you've done enough of that. Sit down and let's enjoy ourselves together. Sit down, my kindred, and may all good fortune sit beside you. If only Semen was here, he'd know how to coax you and make you eat and drink. Nikolay,[8] do you remember how he broke a bottle of whiskey over your head and threw stuffed dumplings out to the dogs because you wouldn't drink with him?"

"Yes, grandma, there was no joking with grandpa. It was either drink or die."

"I will drink to you, Toma, because you're the dearest to me. I want to get drunk. Grandma doesn't need much to make her start singing silly girlish songs. Ah, Toma, my Toma, if I could only be your age again! Go ahead and drink. Don't cast your eyes under the table. If you would only turn them upward instead of downward, your soul would be much relieved. Drink to your uncle Nikolay."

[5] Colloquial for Simon, Simeon.

[6] This story is factual. The widow bears some traits of Stefanyk's grandmother, a great matriarch who sought in vain to save four Basarabs from this fate.

[7] Colloquial for Theodosia.

[8] Nicholas.

102

She stood in front of the table, tall, erect and hoary. Her eyes were large, grey, intelligent. With them she looked out as if there was not a single nook in the whole world unknown to her, or one in which she, having rolled up her long white sleeves, could not do what any competent housekeeper does – tidy the place up, make it spotless, and put everything in its proper order.

"Grandma, it's so good to be here: plenty to eat and drink! And though you say little, your eyes beg us to have our fill."

"That's just the way I am. I have eyes for smiling and making merry. They were not made for tears. My mother did not fashion them so bright for me to dim them by weeping. If you could only drive that dismal fog that darkens the world out of your own eyes! My eyes look upon my children, my land, my cattle and granaries, so why should they be covered with worry? When worry comes, I have a good cry, blubber and snivel, then wipe my tears away, and that's the end to it!"

"Everyone's nature is not the same, grandma. There are those who weep though you feed them honey. Even if you turn them loose in a green field on the finest spring day, they still weep."

"O you Basarabs, you Basarabs! You have no children, no sown fields, not even cattle.[9] You only have clouds, wall-eyes, and long black hair which shuts the sun away from you. God is punishing you because you should be looking at His sun, rejoicing in your children, and stroking your happy cheeks with green blades of grain. Toma, go ahead and eat, and don't get angry at grandma. When you were a baby grandma carried you to be christened. She wept when we were seeing you off to the army, and she clanked the beads of her necklace at your wedding.[10] Grandma is not your enemy. As for your trying to commit suicide, I am really angry at you for that. But first eat what I've cooked for you, because I don't want my labour to go to waste. After that we'll talk.

"My upright and splendid offspring! I rejoice in you more than in anything else, because you do not forget me. You love me, and sit at my table drinking, speaking beautiful words!"

A ripple of joy lit up the faces of the guests, like sunbeams shimmering on dark, deep waters of a lake. All eyes were raised and turned on grandma.

"Ah, Basarabs! Just look, just look at all those eyes, and all of them so full of grief and sadness!"

"Grandma, don't say that, because we're all as pleased with

9 What is meant is that they do not enjoy it all, although they do have them.
10 A custom.

your words as if we had tasted sweet wine. And listen, grandma, we would like to take you to our homes, each in his turn, so that we might enjoy your company."

"Am I, at my age, to gladden your homes? And where are your wives? Are they not blooming? Don't they embroider your shirts, don't they wash your children's heads? You don't see anything, and you don't because you are blind. God has punished you with blindness."

"Grandma, how about us getting up and lighting our pipes? Why sit at the table when our stomachs are full?"

"Then get up, get up and have your smoke. I'm going to sit down beside Toma and ask him what kind of burden is oppressing his soul."

III

Toma was a small lean man with long black hair which fell in soft smooth waves upon his broad forehead. Under it, his jet-black eyes wandered as over endless plains, unable to find their way. His swarthy childlike face was filled with fear. He shoved himself out from behind the table and sat down beside Semen's old widow.

"Go ahead and tell us, Toma, why you find it so hard to live, why you want to forsake your children, your wife and your relations? Don't be ashamed; just tell us all about the venom that's eating away at you. Perhaps we'll be able to give you some advice or help you in some way."

All turned to Toma.

"Tell us, tell us, don't hide anything. You'll feel much relieved if you let us know."

"There isn't anything to hide," replied Toma. "I hid it for as long as I could, but now you know all about it."

"But we don't know anything. You tell us. And if you don't, we'll think that your wife isn't good to you, that your children haven't turned out well, or that we've done you some wrong. Have some consideration for us. You know that when one in our family commits suicide, he at once drags another after him. Perhaps there is already one among us who, hearing of your sad case, has also decided to do away with himself."

It was grey-haired Les[11] who said that.

The Basarabs lowered their heads, as if they were all guilty.

"Todoska, do be quiet, don't cry, stop it."

11 Colloquial for Oles, Alexander.

"I don't know from where or how those thoughts come that give one no peace. You try to think about something else, but they won't let you. You open your eyes wide to chase them away, and yet they howl about your head like dogs. When all is well, my dear ones, no one puts a halter around his neck."

"But when you feel such confusion in your head, why not tell your wife about it, why not go to church?"

"It's no use, grandma. When they surround me, they don't let me take a step from the spot where they want to tie me. If you only knew, if you only knew! They bind me so tight that I feel there are no other chains on earth that could penetrate so deep. And I hear them clash beside me – clink-clank, clink-clank! When they begin clashing, my head splits apart, my ears, it seems, open up like my mouth, so eager are they to hear that clashing sound. At night I turn over and shut one ear only to have the other open up and grind the bones in my head. I cover myself with a pillow, and it still keeps walloping the pillow with those chains. It seems to say, as if gently slipping the words right into my head with a spade: 'Come, come with me. You'll feel so well with me, so very well!' I grasp the bed and hold on to it so tight that the flesh on my hands cracks, as if it was being torn apart alive."

"But why do you say such things, and why do you recall them?" cried his wife.

"Don't be frightened, wife, because they have now completely turned away from me, and I feel as light as if I were just born into the world. But I want to tell you about the tortures of the one who is about to commit suicide. Such a person must be saved, because while he's still alive the fiend is probing him to get hold of his soul, simply piercing him to snatch it out. The evil thing tears your flesh, pries your bones apart, so as to bore holes for itself to get at your soul and clutch it. Such suffering, such fear, such pain does one feel that to get rid of all that agony one would give his hand or foot to be cut off."

"How does it watch you at night? Where does it seize you?"

"One knows ahead of time that it will come, and it doesn't ask whether it is day or night, sunny or cloudy. You simply get up in the morning, say your prayers and start for the yard. You pause on the doorstep and feel as if you've been turned into stone. The sun is shining, people are already shouting beside their cottages, but you keep standing rigid. Why are you standing there? You are standing because something has poked you on the side of the head, and not too gently either. From the head it passes into the throat, and from the throat into the eyes and forehead. Then you immediately know that from beyond the mountains, from beyond the clear sky, even from behind the sun itself, a black cloud will come floating. You can't tell how you know it will come, but for about three days you keep listening to its roar before it crashes across the sky. All your senses leave you as you follow it, and your reason runs away from you like a shepherd forsaking his sheep, and exactly like them you are left all alone. The terror is so great you're afraid to say a single word. Your teeth are clenched and you just wait."

"I know, Toma, I understand. That's exactly the way it comes," said Nikolay Basarab.

"Nikolay! Have you gone crazy or what's come over you?"

"I just said it. There's nothing to it."

The Basarabs looked at Nikolay suspiciously and became silent.

"Folks, don't be afraid of what Toma is relating, because when he tells you all he felt, you'll know how the thing steals up to a baptized soul. It's because your great-great-grandfather killed seven small children when he was warring with the Turks. He pierced them like chicks with his spear. And God punished him, for he immediately ceased to fight and roamed about with those children for thirty years. That is, he didn't really roam about with them, because they mouldered away, but he always carried the spear, and it always seemed to him that he was carrying those children on it. For that reason this punishment fell upon the Basarabs. Even when I was about to marry Semen, my mother told me about this and advised me not to. And now you're doing penance for that sin, for those children. But it crops up among you only now and then. Not every Basarab carries this sin; God places it only on the conscience of some particular one. But don't be frightened by that. Just as Toma says, keep in mind that sin tramples a man until he is redeemed. The body endures everything and, outwardly, seems none the worse for it, but conscience does torment the mind. How it is, is plainly seen if, for example, you take a tree, one so tall that it almost reaches the clouds. Cleave it in two, and all you see is a worm-eaten hollow, but no worm. You won't see it at all, and yet the tree inside has been eaten out completely. So does conscience gnaw at a man from generation to generation."

"Conscience does torment a man, and that is a punishment greater than all the others."

"Tell us all about it, Toma. How does it torture you? It can't be helped now, we must hear you out to the very end."

"It tortures but doesn't say why. For if I killed someone or set a place on fire, it would see me do it. But I'm not guilty, and it still punishes me. And so, when such a cloud crashes across the sky, then comes the exact moment for one to commit suicide. You walk near a body of water and it draws you. How it kisses you, hugs you, caresses your forehead! And your forehead is like glowing embers, like blazing coals! You just have an urge to leap into that water as if it were heaven itself. But from somewhere in your head a word comes to the surface: run, run, run! As if with countless horses it drives you away from that water, drawing all the breath out of your chest, and your head is just splitting apart, because it is going mad. Now at last it does go mad. You glance at a willow tree, and you are stopped again. Your hands become so happy they bustle with excitement, without any effort on your part, without your will, of their own accord. They seize the branches, trying, testing their strength, while you seem to be standing aside, as if it weren't you but your hands alone that were doing it. And again the word comes rushing up: run, run! Your hands feel as though sprayed with fire and fall to your sides as if withered, and again you run. If your eyes light on anyone, a woman or a child, the voice shouts: run! It also speaks and smiles to them, but always in such a way as if it isn't you who is speaking. And the thing drives you to a place where there are no people. You reach a point where you are recalling a pear tree you haven't seen since childhood. Where there is a peg, where there is a hook, where there is some sort of a joist – you recall everything. It drives a man a thousand ways at once, but he doesn't know where to go. And then it leaves you, it leaves you suddenly. An hour will pass, or even two, or even a day, and then again it comes. The heart grows frigid, the eyes weep, weep as if they were trickling out. But neither are the tears seen nor the weeping heard. Once more it drives you along and tortures you all over again. More than once did I drink a whole quart of whiskey and swallow one pepper after another so that it would gnaw itself out, but nothing helped.

"But yesterday it finally smothered me so that I lost all control of my reason, eyes and hands. It came right at noontime. When it came, it pointed out to me the joist in the granary. It showed me every tiny bit of it, every knot in it. I didn't even resist, because there was no way out. I simply untied the rope from the manger and climbed up into the granary. I felt so peaceful, so light. I was tying the rope and testing whether it held well, knowing all the while how to make a noose and how high it should be drawn up. Today I'm surprised at myself and how peacefully and joyfully I was trying to commit suicide. But now, thank God, it has left me, and I'm so very, very glad."

The Basarabs seemed benumbed in a trance-like dream.

"It's our sins, folks, our sins. We must implore God to forgive our sins."

"The doctors say there is a certain nerve, and that it gets sick just like a man. It's somewhere in him, and when it gets sick, it takes away his reason."

"Bah! What do the doctors know!"

IV

"Hey! Go out and see where Nikolay has gone," said Semen's widow.

The Basarabs shuddered, but not one moved from his place. They seemed petrified.

"Well, go out and see where Nikolay is, I say. Where has he gone?"

The women raised a lament. The Basarabs leaped up and all at once rushed into the yard.

"Quiet! Be quiet! No one knows as yet what happened. So don't start screaming. . . ."

The Thief

Two powerful, sturdy men stood in the middle of the room. Their shirts were torn, and their faces were stained with blood.

"Don't ever think, my fellow, that I'll let you out of my grip."

Both were tired. They were panting and gasping for air. A young wife stood leaning against the bed, sleepy and frightened.

"Don't stand there but go and get Mikhaylo[1] and Maksim.[2] Tell them to come at once because I have a thief in my clutches."

The wife went out and they remained alone.

"If this fellow had stumbled on a weakling, he'd have taken the man's life, right by his victim's cottage."

He walked over to the bench, lifted the jug of water and drank so greedily that one could hear the water gurgling down his throat. Then he wiped his face with his sleeve and, looking at the thief, said:

"It won't be necessary to go to a barber;[3] this one has bled me enough."

He had hardly finished saying this when the thief struck him between the eyes with his fist.

"You bash me, eh? Well, I'll bash you too. Let's see who can do it better."

He swung a stout beechen log in the air and the thief fell to the floor, blood spurting from his legs.

"Now try and escape if you can. I won't object."

They were silent for a long time. The dim light from the small oil lamp was unable to pierce the darkness in the corners of the room. Flies began to buzz timidly.

"Man, stanch the blood or it will all drain out of you."

"Give me some water, chum."

"I'll give you some water. Refresh yourself, because you don't know what's in store for you."

A long silence followed.

"As I found out, you're pretty strong."

"I am strong, my poor fellow. I can lift a horse on my shoulders. It was unlucky for you to cross my path."

"But aren't you kind?"

"I am kind, but I never let a thief get out of my hands alive."

"Then, am I to die here?"

"How should I know whether you're hard or soft? If you're hard, you might be able to stand it."

Silence again began to reign in that room with a low ceiling.

"Stanch that blood."

"Why? So that it'll hurt me more when you beat me? The blood is the worst cause of pain."

---

1 Colloquial for Mikhail, Michael.

2 Colloquial for Maximius or Maximian.

3 In those days a barber usually practiced blood-letting as a means of curing a patient.

"When I start beating you, you're bound to feel pain until you breathe your last."

"And will you have no fear of God in you?"

"And did you fear God when you sneaked into my larder? All that I've gained in my life is there. If you had taken it, you would have crippled me for ever and a day. Why don't you creep up on a rich man, instead of on one who is poor?"

"It's too late now. No use talking about it. Beat me and be done with it all."

"Of course, I'm going to beat you."

A pool of blood had formed on the floor.

"If you have a conscience, friend, don't go killing me bit by bit, but take that log once more and bash me over the head with it, as you did across my legs. That way you'll get rid of your trouble, and it will be easier for me."

"You'd like it to be done at once! Hold on, wait, be patient till the men come."

"So you want to prepare a ball for your good neighbours?"

"Here they come."

* * *

"Glory to Christ!"[4]

"Glory for ever!"[4]

"What's happened at your place Gyorgiy?"[5]

"Something has happened alright. A guest has come, and we must entertain him."

"No question about it. We must."

Mikhalyo and Maksim almost filled the whole room; their heads just about touched the ceiling, and their hair reached the middle of their backs.

"Sit down, and forgive me for spoiling the night for you."

"Is that him on the floor?"

"That's him."

"A man as huge as a beast! You must have had trouble enough hauling him into the house."

"He's strong. My, he's strong. Only he came upon one stronger still. But before we start anything, sit down at the table and invite the guest to do the same."

[4] Conventional religious salutation and response.

[5] Colloquial for George. In Ukrainian the name is usually Yuriy or Yurko. The letter 'g' is to be pronounced hard.

Gyorgiy went out and in a while returned with a bottle of whiskey, salted pork and bread.

"Why don't you place him at the table too?"

"He says he can't get up."

"Then I'll help him."

The host took hold of the thief under the armpits and seated him at the table.

You've already had an argument with him in the house, eh, Gyorgiy?"

"Yes, he wanted to knock me senseless. When he walloped me between the eyes, let me tell you, I was about ready to fall down, but I happened to touch a small log near at hand and whacked him across the legs, and he just dropped on the spot and remained stock-still."

"Don't be surprised at him. Everyone wants to protect himself."

"Well, I'm not blaming him."

The thief sat at the table, pale and apathetic; Maksim sat beside him, and farther on, Mikhaylo. Gyorgiy's wife, in her sheepskin coat, stood beside the clay-stove.

"Gyorgiy, what do you mean to do with him? Men, bring him to his senses. He wants to kill a human being!"

"Wife, I can see you're frightened. Go to mother's and stay there overnight. You can come back tomorrow."

"I won't leave the house."

"Then you'll have to drink with us. And no screaming, or you'll get it good and hard from me. Climb up onto the clay-stove and go to sleep, or look on. Whatever you wish."

She did not stir from the stove.

"A woman's a woman, Gyorgiy. She's just as scared of a fight as a Jew, so don't be surprised."

"Bah! Why take any notice of her? Good health, my man. I'll drink to you. I only wonder who's going to commit a sin for who: you for me or I for you? But sin there must be. It just so happened that sin cannot be avoided. Go ahead, drink."

"I don't want to."

"When I ask you to do me that favour, you've got to! Whiskey will bring you a bit to, because you're all limp and seedy."

"I don't want to get drunk with you."

The three peasants turned toward the thief; their relentless black eyes predicted his end.

"Pass it over then, and let me drink, but five glasses at once."

"Drink. If we run short, we'll send for more."

He kept on filling his glass till he drank six portions. Then Mikhaylo and Maksim had their drinks. They snacked on the food and drank again.

Mikhaylo asked:

"Tell us, man, where have you tramped into our village from? Are you from near or far?"

"From here, there, and everywhere."

"Tell us, then, do you belong to our muzhik breed, to the city folk, or to the gentry? Because we are going to deal with you accordingly. This is how one beats up a muzhik: about three whacks on the head with a wagon bar[6] and several clouts in the face, so as to knock him down. The muzhik is tough and one has to deal hard with him. Once he's under your foot, the rest is easy. On the other hand, a man of the upper class is treated in a different manner: you don't even let him see the end of the bar, or he'd die at once; you simply frighten him with a whiphandle. And when he's shivering all over, just strike him a couple of times in the mug, not too hard at that, and he's already under your foot. Trample him for a minute or two, and he's finished; his ribs are crushed like dry branches – his are delicate bones, as white as paper. When you get a Jew, you first of all take hold of his side-curls. He jumps, spits, and squirms like a spring. But you pay no attention to that; you simply put your thumb between your first and second fingers and jab him in the ribs, and keep jabbing. This kind of brawl is easy, but very painful to him."

The peasants burst into hard dull laughter. Mikhaylo thrust his head behind Maksim and waited to hear what the thief would say to him.

"Well, which party do you join?"

"It's as simple as this, my friend: if you keep on drinking whiskey, you'll never let me out of your clutches alive."

"You speak the truth. By God, it's the truth! I like you for that."

"But before you kill me, give me more whiskey so that I can get so drunk as not to know when and how it happens."

"Drink! If it's for that reason, then drink. I don't mind. But, God smite you down! why did you have to meet one like me? Take my word for it – I'm hard, hard as stone; no one will wrench you out of my hands."

[6] One of several bars, usually wooden, used to support the rack of a wagon in which hay or straw is carted.

The thief drank five more glasses of whiskey.

"Now beat me as much as you like. I'm ready."

"Wait a minute, man, it's all very well that you're satisfied, but we're not. You've been drinking five to our one. When we catch up to you, then we'll begin to talk business."

Mikhaylo looked quite pleased; Maksim was thinking about something, but was afraid to reveal it, and Gyorgiy was restless.

"Men, I see trouble ahead, and I'd like to get out of it altogether; but something is pulling me to him, as if with chains. What can I do about it? Come, let's drink and eat."

"Friend, let me kiss your hand," said the thief to Maksim.

"So that's it! Are you frightened so much? Shame on you. That's not nice."

"Honest, of you I'm not afraid. Honest to God! I can swear a hundred times that I'm not afraid of you."

"Then what?"

"My soul feels such relief now that I would like to kiss this good man's hand. His hair is grey. He could be my father."

"Man, leave me alone. I have a tender conscience, so leave me alone. You'll do better without me."

"Just give me your hand, or you'll commit a sin if you don't. I want to kiss your hand, as if you were my own father."

"I'm too soft-hearted. I don't want you to kiss my hand."

Mikhaylo and Gyorgiy stopped drinking and sat with their mouths wide open. Their hair bristled, and they could hardly believe their ears.

"He's pulling the wool over our eyes. What's he up to? So that's your game, eh? Well, we, too, are wise to that."

Maksim stared like a ram, at a loss to understand what was happening.

"It occurred to him that I was kind-hearted. He must have guessed it at once."

He said that in order to justify himself before Mikhaylo and Gyorgiy.

"Give me your hand, give me your hand, friend, out of the kindness of your heart, and when I kiss it, I'll feel better. I realize that I'm not long for this world, and that's why I'd like to beg your forgiveness."

"Don't kiss my hand, or I'll get much too soft. I forgive you anyway."

"But I beg you. I'm going to die a hard death, and I have

never kissed anyone's hand, that is, not with a heart-felt delight. I'm not drunk, honest I'm not. I just want to kiss it, and that is all."

"Be quiet! Stop jabbering, and don't try to put anything over us, or I'll clout you so hard you won't even wriggle."

"You still think I'm fooling you. Really, I'm telling you the honest truth. You see, after having a few drinks of whiskey, it suddenly became clear in my head that I have to die, and that I must kiss this man's hand so that God would make my sins lighter. Come, give me your hand, friend. Tell him to give it to me."

"What does the man want of me when I can't help matters? Yet, I'm so soft-hearted that I can't stand it."

Maksim did not know what to do with himself in such a perplexity. He was as embarrassed as a girl.

"That's always the case with a soft-hearted man. He's always a laughingstock to others on account of such a disgusting nature in him. I start weeping after I've had a few drinks, you know that very well. You shouldn't have asked me to come here because you know that I'm like spun yarn."

The thief wanted to take Maksim's hand and kiss it.

"This thief wants to get the best of us by trickery. Go, Maksim, get away from him altogether."

"Give us whiskey, Gyorgiy, let's drink at least three more glasses each to get our dander up," said Mikhaylo.

"Don't go, Maksim, don't go away from me, crony, or I'll die here and now. I'm not afraid, honest I'm not, but I feel such a painful irritation in me that. . . ."

His whole body began to tremble, and his lips quivered as if they were palsied. Mikhaylo and Gyorgiy paid no attention to him but went on drinking.

"Why are you so scared? There's no reason to be frightened. I'll give you my hand to kiss even if they beat me up for it. Don't worry, I'll give it to you. Here, kiss it if that's what you want."

The thief clung to the offered hand while Maksim was blinking as if he were being struck intermittent blows across the face.

"A man should never be so kind-hearted, because then he's worthless and good for nothing."

Mikhaylo spread out the fingers of both his hands and showed them to Gyorgiy.

"Look, man! Such strong fingers, and as eager for a fight as could be; wherever they grab they tear the flesh."

Gyorgiy made no reply but kept on spitting into his hands and pouring whiskey.

"Enough, you poor fellow, enough. Let go my hand and I'll leave. I see that God is not to be found here. I can't bear to look at all that. Get your hands out of my shirt and don't go feeling me all over. Let go, because I'm so ashamed I don't know what to do with myself."

"I also want to kiss the holy pictures, even the doorstep. In fact, everyone, everyone in the world!" cried the thief.

The housewife jumped down from the clay-stove and fled. Mikhaylo came out from behind the table, drunk and sombre as night. Gyorgiy was standing, trying to recall what it was he had to do.

"Maksim, get out of my house, and don't let me see you here again, or I'll kill you like a sparrow. Now, clear out."

"I'll go, Gyorgiy, I don't mind going. Yet, you mustn't be angry at me, because you know I'm a soft-hearted man. But it seems you're about to commit a sin. I'm leaving now."

"Go, go! You're not a man but a slobbering old woman."

"Well, I've been trying to tell you that I'm not for this kind of business, I. . . ."

Maksim got up and edged himself out from behind the table.

"Goodbye, and don't hold this against me, because I am, as someone has said, not for this kind of business."

The thief alone was left behind the table. He was somewhat pale, but cheerful.

"Are you going to come out from behind the table, or will we have to carry you out?"

"I won't come out. I'm sure I won't come out, because I have to sit right here below the holy pictures."

"Oh yes, you will. By God, you'll come out. We're going to invite you to come out of there."

And they pounced on him like hungry wolves.

My Word

With pale lips and in undertones, I will tell you about myself. No complaint, no joy or sadness hear in this my word!

I went away from my mother in a white shirt, myself as white.

They laughed at my white shirt. They wronged and wounded me.

And I walked my quiet way like a white kitten.

I felt the baseness of my silent course, and blood dript from my childlike heart.

And I slept in a rented house, among wretched human hulks permeated with ill-repute.[1]

Like a tiny leaf of white birch on a rubbish-heap.

* * *

I discarded the homespun shirt my mother made for me. The world of my childhood and the long line of my peasant ancestors were left behind.

Before me stood a new world – new and ominous.

I clutched at its lapels, and it looked down upon me with contempt.

As if I were a little beggar.

I was stricken mute with pain. And I was silent for many, many years.

My words remained unuttered, my lamentation unfinished, and my laughter incomplete!

They pressed me down as the black stones of a broken cross press upon a grave in a foreign land!

* * *

I found friends.

They had become reconciled to the new world. I spoke to them of the world I had forsaken, and of the new one which wronged us.

They said that I lied.

But I kept struggling on, falling into a mire when strength failed, yet persevering.

Once more they said I was a liar. And they abandoned me.

And when I wept, my mother sobbed:

[1] While attending the gymnasium at Kolomiya, without being aware of it, Stefanyk, for a time, lived in a house of public women.

"Stay where you are. The rich will not accept you. You should not have left me."

And I remained like a clump of willows out in the field.

* * *

I sat amidst the fields.

My thoughts spun themselves into long furrows, like those of a fertile soil. They sucked the earth and nurtured me with loneliness.

They also brought me salty sweat and gentle songs unfurling themselves behind the tiller, the plow and him who drove the oxen. They filled me with the peace that muses above yokes of oxen at the plow.

I likewise saw tiny camp-fires among little shepherds, and sheep in the fields.

Here, like a mighty wind, I will reign and sing my song!

* * *

I created a world for myself.

On my right, the blue field, black furrows, shiny plow, song and salty sweat.

And on my left, the sinister machine, groaning curses out of its crimson mouth.

But in my heart my world is woven with silk, embroidered with silver white, and strewn about with pearls.

So it is in my own kingdom.

* * *

I will carve my world as I would a rock.

I will sharpen my word on the flintstone of my soul, and, having steeped it in poisonous herbs, I will cast it to the left.

And I will shatter my word into lustrous sunbeams, dip it into every little flower, and scatter it to the right.

Always will I sculpture my rock, always! Until I place it on my grave like a lifeless beauty.

And the cherry tree at my head will take all my heartaches for its blossoms.

* * *

And in my world I live. In it I live indeed!

Like one possessed, I wade through the clouds of my own phantasy.

Countless times I send forth the forces of my soul to seek out my happiness in distant worlds.

On the placid lake of my past float the nets of my ardent desires, striving to capture all the bright moments of my life.

But the nets break asunder, unable to snatch anything.

They return to me tired and wanting – as peasants from a field.

And in sadness I am dreaming in the clouds.

* * *

But when the thunder crashes, again my forehead is lifted up.

I fly, I fly on sombre clouds.

With a golden arrow I pierce the luminous heights.

The stars hide themselves in my black hair as in a dark cloud.

From my eyes the cold clouds descend as warm rain upon the earth.

But I am unable to reach the sun.

And I fall down from the lofty heights.

As an old soldier staggers along on wooden legs, so stagger I.

* * *

When my wings are healed, once more I soar to the sun, to happiness.

Again I cleave the heavenly spheres, and again I fall.

* * *

I used to be happy.

When, as a child, I gazed into my mother's eyes as over them, ever so softly, crept impeccable cloudlets of joy – I was happy.

But now the hand of death has placed its palm upon those eyes.

While I continue to seek happiness beneath heaven, and fall time and again. . . .

The Trial

Kovaliuk lifted a neck-yoke high in the air and addressed the musicians:

"Play your best, make it sound the way it should, because this wedding is going to be famous throughout the entire Ukraine, in Kolomiya[1] and in Stanislaw[1]. . . .

"This one doesn't need a wedding any longer, but there are still two who will have to dance."

He was pointing to Fedko[2] Prodan who was lying in the snow with his head split open. His wife was sitting beside him, holding a new hat in her hands and asking:

"What do you want me to do now? Is there anything you'd like me to say to the children?"

She also spoke to him about other things, as if she were sending a message to the other world.

Dmitro[3] Zolotiy walked back and forth in front of the gate with a piece of thick wagon-reach in his hands, threatening the crowd on the street:

"Let no one dare step this way or he'll be put to sleep at once with this here thing. I'm warning you."

"Who are they beating up?"

"The rich guys."

"Who's doing the beating?"

"The wedding guests."

"Have they killed Fedko already?"

"Right now he's on the other shore."

"It's death for him, and jail for who?"

The village bell began to sound an alarm.

"The villagers will be here in a moment and won't let this go on," someone ventured.

"They will, they will!" cried Zolotiy. "They'll just hang around here like you."

A fresh scuffle broke out near the porch. Mikhaylo Pecheniuk stuck his hands and feet against the doorposts and neither Petrik[4] Sinitsia nor both the Zolotiys — Ivan and Kalenik[5] — were able to drag him out.

"You underfed weaklings!" shouted Pecheniuk. "I'm strong; I eat meat every day while you live on hasty-pudding."

"You'll bite the dust when we're through with you."

A burst of hysterical weeping was heard from the women in the porch. It sounded like a red echo.

1 Towns in the southern part of the province of Galicia, in Western Ukraine.
2 Colloquial for Theodore.
3 Colloquial for Demetrius.
4 Diminutive for Petro, Peter.
5 Colloquial for Callinicus.

"Don't say that to them, Mikhaylo, don't say that! Beg, plead with them," wailed his wife.

"What do you know, you silly woman? There's no pleading here, there's only death!"

As they were arguing, Petrik Sinitsia seized Mikhaylo's finger between his teeth and pulled him out in a trice.

"That's that! Now it's amen for Mikhaylo."

Someone shouted to Mikhaylo's wife: "Sit on his head. The head is the main part to protect."

"You trying to give advice? I'll advise you with this club."

"Blood is gushing out of him as out of a stuck pig, such rich blood."

"Just look. He's crossing himself, and they're beating him; they won't even let him finish saying his prayers."

"It's all over with him now. His wife is placing a candle in his hands, but it's not lighted."

"What if he was strong? He's mud now, and that's that!"

"His wife isn't weeping a bit; she's all in."

A group of women, with Kassian in their midst, came rushing out of the porch. Sinitsia and both the Zolotiys started after them.

"You won't hide yourself behind women's skirts, you wealthy brute."

The women formed a thick wall around Kassian.

"Don't let them get me, don't let them!"

"Poor Kassian is scared, but he must be drubbed more than the others. He's the meanest of the rich ones around here."

"He's scared alright; he's not like Mikhaylo. That one wasn't afraid."

"Look what a nuisance those women are! Just look at them spitting at the Zolotiys!"

"They've seized Petrik Sinitsia and have all piled on top of him."

"They won't give up Kassian."

"Why are you butting in from out there? You're good at beating your wives or shaking Jews by their side-curls, but when it comes right down to business, you stand far apart and yelp like puppies," said one of the women who was defending Kassian to those who stood by and looked on.

"How about you, reeve, why don't you go and restore order? Can't you see that women are doing your work?"

"You're smart, aren't you? Go ahead, reeve, go ahead and croak, just because hoodlums have made up their minds to beat up the rich!"

The day dawned and the houses stood out in the snow like a flock of huge black birds. The forest murmured most peacefully. The bell was still sounding an alarm.

Ivan Zolotiy's wife came out from the crowd, seized her blood-bespattered husband by the sleeve and said:

"Man! Look around at those people, at the village, at the forest, and come to your senses. What have you done? People are human beings, not cattle."

Behind her came Kalenik Zolotiy's wife and said to her husband:

"You go straight to jail. Don't ever come to the house, or I'll take the children and leave. Don't you dare come!"

The musicians stopped playing, and Kovaliuk stood there with a whiffle-tree, not knowing what to do with it. The sun was displaying half of its golden eye.

The three Zolotiys threw down their clubs and hoes and went into the forest. Kovaliuk began to weep, and Petrik Sinitsia was on the way to his cottage, but, having reached it, he fell on the doorstep and foamed at the mouth. The crowd came to life and began to remove the dead.

II

The villagers were about to try the killers in the home of Onufriy[6] Melnyk. None of the wealthy were allowed to be present at the trial – the sentence was to be passed by the poor peasants alone. Onufriy appointed the entire court of justice, including the prosecution and defence. He himself was seated behind a table and began thus:

"Our village has become poisoned. People are afraid of one another. Every Sunday the whole sermon in church is all about the bad things poor people do. Gendarmes scurry about the village, and the bells announce the arrival of all kinds of commissions. They root up graves, rip people, cut them open. And for us poor wretches there is no help, not even a kind word. Let's try these killers ourselves, and if we find them guilty, we'll punish them."

Thus spoke Onufriy to all the poor people. Almost everyone in the village had turned out to witness the trial. They filled the house, packed around the clay-stove and bed, crowded the hallway and the yard.

6 Onuphrius.

Onufriy continued: "And if the reeve should come along and want to disperse us, don't let him. If he tries to force his way in, give him a few slaps in the face and let him run. And now, our honoured Prosecutor, please tell us all about the charge."

Yakiv[7] Didyk arose from the bench and began:

"Ivan Zub, a poor man, had a wedding for his daughter, as you all know. You also know how it is with a common peasant – he's always glad to have the rich come, because when a rich man enters, the holy pictures take on a brighter glow – you see, there's someone of importance to sit below them. The poor peasants were all at the wedding. But Zub had also invited three rich men: Fedko Melnyk, Mikhaylo Pecheniuk and Kassian Kropivka. 'Good health to you'; 'may you live long'; 'thank you for dropping into my house and making this wedding the merrier for me.' In this fashion Zub continued fawning on the rich, while the poor neglected devils pressed silently together about the threshold and doorposts and listened. All one could hear was – 'at your service'; 'will you be so good as to'; 'help yourself'; 'have a taste of this' – but always to the rich. And the rich, if you please, kept on drinking and pushing the ordinary peasants farther away from the table and toward the bed. And Zub had forgotten about his simple guests and waited only on rich. This is the first point.

"Then Petrik Sinitsia spoke out: 'You, Zub, you, old man, must have forgotten that there are other guests here, not only these three.'

"And Zub, already under the influence, replied: 'Sinitsia, my dear fellow, don't start laying down the law as to how I'm to act in my own home. I'll do as I please.'

" 'Oh, no you won't! I came to the wedding as did the others, I brought my gifts as did the others, therefore I should have the same respect as the others.'

"As Sinitsia was saying this, the peasants pricked up their ears and listened eagerly. Those words were as sweet as honey to them. And that's how matters stood for the time being.

"The dinner was served. Salted pork and cooked meat with just a little corn mush was placed before the rich, but only a little meat and a heaping pile of corn mush was put before the plain peasants. The poor fellows showed their displeasure, some eating a bit and some not at all, while the rich gorged themselves till they had grease on their arms and elbows.

[7] Jacob, James.

"Then Ivan Zolotiy took the bottle of whiskey from in front of the rich and said: 'Brothers, if they're not going to give us anything to eat, let's at least drink.'

" 'For goodness sake, Zolotiy, what about the food that's placed before you? Isn't it God's gift?' asked Zub.

" 'But how come so many of God's gifts are placed before the rich, and so few before us?'

"The rich got red in the face. All they did was glance around slyly, but said nothing.

"The supper was over and the musicians began to play. The dance was on. Then Pecheniuk began to caper with Kassian's wife and started bumping and pushing others about. Petrik couldn't stand it any longer and whacked Mikhaylo in the face, and before you could count up to three, Mikhaylo slapped Petrik in return.

" 'Halt! Stop playing!' yelled Zub.

"Then Kassian said to Zub: 'You know what, Zub! Here's fifty *levs* for you. I'm paying for the whole wedding, but you've got to sweep all this rubbish out of the house.' This is the second point.

"It came to such a pass that someone's life had to face death. Horrors! When Kalenik Zolotiy walloped Kassian in the mouth, a bowlful of blood soon gushed out. Then Mikhaylo seized Kalenik by the scruff of the neck and tore off some skin, exposing raw flesh.

" 'Hey, you rich ones! Either get out of here or stay and be smashed to smithereens!' yelled Kalenik.

"If they had only taken the hint, all would have been well.

"The tussle then began in all earnest. Those with little courage ran away, and only the three rich peasants, five poor ones, and the women were left. The women stayed, knowing that no one strikes them when a fight is on. The first one to be led out was Fedko Melnyk. He was dragged out by Kovaliuk, Petrik and Ivan. Kovaliuk banged him over the head just once with a whiffle-tree; the skull split open at once, and Fedko fell into his last sleep on the spot, like a chick.

"It wasn't such an easy matter to deal with Mikhaylo Pecheniuk. As you all know, he was as strong as a bear, and certainly not timid. They tangled with him in the house for about three hours – four of them against him alone. True, the women helped him, but they couldn't do much. The men got him down on the floor – he threw them off like dumplings; they got him down in the hallway – again he fought them off; they dragged him to the door – he seized the doorframe and they couldn't budge him. Then Petrik Sinitsia snapped Pecheniuk's finger between his teeth and pulled him out. And when they had him outside, he was clubbed to death. Those that did the killing are Petrik, Kalenik and Ivan. They also wanted to kill Kassian, but, in the first place, he pleaded with the women, and they protected him between their long skirts, and, in the second place, the day dawned and the people came to their senses.

"Those who did the killing are Ivan, Kalenik, and Dmitro Zolotiys,[8] Petrik Sinitsia, and Nikifir[9] Kovaliuk."

"You have heard the prosecutor give the details of the charge, and now we'll hear from the accused," said Onufriy.

"Ivan Zolotiy."

"Present."

"Are you guilty of killing Mikhaylo Pecheniuk and Fedko Melnyk?"

"No, not guilty."

"Then who is guilty?"

"Not us. The rich are to blame."

"Why the rich?"

"They are to blame because they wanted to drive us away from the wedding."

"They wanted to, but you resisted, and sent them to the other world."

"Well, why ask me about it?"

"Now, Ivan, shut up, you snake. Don't get too smart with me or you'll catch it right now. Tell us, did you do the killing?"

At this point the villagers who thronged the room began to help Onufriy:

"You Zolotiy, tell the whole truth, or you'll get a sound cudgeling this very moment."

"Honest to God, I hit him only once."

"With what?"

"With a hoe."

"Where?"

"Across the shoulders."

"Now then, what did Kalenik do?"

"I don't know."

[8] Three brothers, hence the plural of the surname.
[9] Nicephorus.

124

"If you don't know, sit down."

"Kalenik Zolotiy."

"That's me."

"Did you kill Mikhaylo?"

"His wealth killed him."

"Kalenik, no wisecracks!"

"What do you mean — wisecracks? I was drunk; the wedding feast was in full swing; the music played; the rich ones were about to drive us out, and we wanted to beat them up a bit."

"You certainly did! But who killed Mikhaylo?"

"I don't remember."

"Your memory is somewhat short. What did you hit him with?"

"With whatever I had in my hands."

Onufriy said nothing more. He waved his hand, signaling to the younger men. They took hold of Kalenik.

"Give him fifteen blows with the club and he'll talk."

The investigation continued. The people were all for meting out punishment on the spot, but Onufriy would not allow it. He persisted in questioning the rest of the accused. When they refused to testify before Onufriy, those standing in the hall began to cry out: "They have done the killing, now let them get the penalty they deserve."

They dragged them out one after another and passed them to other hands. And those hands — more than one could count — seized them, took horrible revenge on them, raised a ferocious, roaring outcry through the whole village, leaving in its wake the frightened screams of women and the dying moments of the wave of vengeance.

Mother Earth

When Semen[1] returned home at sunset he found five wagons with iron-rimmed wheels in his yard. They were filled with all manner

1 Diminutive of Simeon or Simon.

of things. There was even a cradle on top of one wagon. Fine looking horses stood beside them. Old and young people, all strangers, sat in a row on the *prizba*[2] in front of the house. Semen, old and barefooted, his shoes slung over his shoulders, said to them:

"Glory to Jesus Christ,[3] good people! Where are you from, and what am I to call you?"

"We are Bukovinians.[4] The war has driven us out of our homes. I am Danilo,[5] and here beside me is my wife, Maria, already senile. And these are my two daughters-in-law with their children, and my daughter, also with her children. We'd like to pass the night in your house, if you will receive us."

"You may stay for the night and be our guests. I'll sit down beside you and we'll have a chat while my wife prepares supper. She's my second one, young, and able when she wants to be."

"This is my first one. She's been married to me for fifty years, and has now gone mad. I'll bury her somewhere at the crossroads, because she's lost her reason beneath the wheels. While she could still see our village from the wagon, she just wept and kept jumping down to the ground. But my daughters-in-law always caught up with her. When she could no longer see her village, she became mute. And here she sits speechless among her grandchildren."

"My friend Danilo, don't be surprised, She has left her words on the windows and on the gilded holy pictures in her home and they, like tiny orphaned birds, are now flinging themselves against the walls of the empty house. They are warbling prayers in all the nooks of the house, and without them the old woman will remain mute. . . . Take her into the large room before the icon of St. Nikolay[6] and say a prayer for her."

The two old men dragged her before the holy pictures and recited a prayer in a loud voice. But she remained silent.

"She lost her words in front of her own saints, and only there will she find them."

Again they were seated on the *prizba*.

"It's not my business to ask, but why have you forsaken your

[2] A clay ledge about a foot in height and width adjacent to the foundations of a peasant's home.

[3] Conventional religious salutation.

[4] Ukrainians from the province of Bukovina in Western Ukraine.

[5] Colloquial for Danyil, Daniel.

[6] Nicholas.

land, and driven away from it in these wagons with iron-rimmed wheels, with such fine horses, and with small children?"

"My friend Semen, I put my children into these fine wagons bound in iron, and with these raven-black horses I fled to preserve my young ones from abuse. When they chained the priest and his wife and carted them off to the mountains, when during the night they took the teacher away, God knows where, when they hanged the reeve in the centre of the village and posted a soldier to prevent anyone from burying him, I renounced my land and into these wagons I packed those of my flesh and blood so that no one would desecrate them. The Tsar is orthodox, and we are orthodox – and that's supposed to be treachery! That is the first reason. The second is that the Muscovites are coming and blocking off the sun from us. From China, from Siberia, from all over the earth wild men are coming to butcher the old, rape our young women and cut off their breasts. Small children are being put into trains and scattered all over the barren lands in distant kingdoms. . . . The windows in the village are in darkness, and the church bells are silenced. The punishment of God has descended upon us for the sins of the whole world. That was why I tried to remove from the heavy hand of the merciful Lord my children, my blood, and bring them into a Christian country."

"They are calling us to supper, Danilo. But listen, don't offend God with your unreasonable grief."

* * *

"Eat, reach out for the food, you birds who fly not knowing where. And we, Danilo, let's both of us have a taste of this bitter liquor. Maybe it will make our old shoulders rise upward from the ground."

The supper was not enjoyed by any of them. Both the old men kept on drinking whiskey, without putting any food into their mouths.

"Go, children, go to sleep with the other little ones, and may God paint bright dreams for you. We oldsters will remain here awhile."

"Danilo, if only you wouldn't get angry at me, I would tell you something."

"Reason and anger I have left behind me, in my yard. You may even beat me, because, as you see, I'm an old bird without a nest."

"Let an old bird not forsake his old nest, because he is no longer able to build a new one. Because it is better that his head stiffen in the old nest than in a gully along some foreign road."

"It's true, Semen, it's true. I thank you for these words."

"And where are you headed to? Are you following the gentry and the Jews? The Emperor's[7] treasury is open to them, but closed to you. When you enter a foreign country, and find yourselves within its cold walls, fate will scatter you over rocky spaces, and only in your dreams will you see your beautiful land. With your hands, numb with cold, you will absent-mindedly sow spring wheat on stony ground. To the gentry who strut about you will become a laughingstock. From among those rocks God will not receive you unto Himself, but He will come to meet you at His very gates if they kill you on your own land. Return to your soft soil, and God will bless you there, even on the gallows."

"I am a sinner, Semen, a sinner before God and before you. Just think! My cultivated fields are like well-fed sheep, black and curly. Right at this moment I'm going to turn my wagons toward the rising sun and offend God no longer."

"Our concern is with the land. If you let her go, you perish; if you hold on to her, she draws out all your strength, scoops up your soul with her palms; if you tend her and become stooped, she pulls out your sinews. But for all that you have herds and flocks and stacks of grain. And in return for your strength she gives you a houseful of children and grandchildren who, with faces red as cranberries, laugh like silver bells. . . . Danilo, don't follow the gentry and the Jews, don't go looking for the Tsar, because you don't need him. Someone or other will always come to the muzhik to collect the taxes. . . ."

"For your counsel, Semen, may God grant you all that is best. I'm going to return home, and let God's will be done."

Then, suddenly, the old woman, Maria, spoke out: "Let's go home, Danilo, let's go home."

"There you are! What a wench! When things turned out her way, she spoke out at once!"

"And now let's drink before we say good-bye. God grant that we may survive these evil times. And when we die, may our bones rot away in our own land."

And, together with the old woman, the two men drank and sang. She sat in the middle, tightly hugging them both and leading them in singing:

1 Austrian.

> *"Only my true love,*
> *Grey-plumed turtle-dove,*
> *Does not lie asleep.*
> *She rocks her child,*
> *Writes letters mild,*
> *And with the mighty wind*
> *A converse she does keep."*

And so they sang until daybreak.

At dawn the iron-rimmed wagons began to rattle. Danilo was getting ready to return home.

When the sun was rising, the old men bade farewell to each other, kissing one another's hands dark from the soil. And the red sun cast their shadows across the boundaries of the fields, far across the land.

Maria

Maria sat on the *prizba*[1] and whispered:

"Would to God that girls were never born into the world! They roam about like bitches. Some are already under the sod, and others are still making merry with the cossacks in taverns. Now, why are they born on God's earth? They're so foolish and shameless, it's no wonder they lose their maidenhood!"

She herself had just hidden her two daughters in a secret underground shelter in the cellar as soon as the alarm spread through the village that a fresh band of cossacks was approaching.

What do those cossacks want? What are they searching for? Her barns are empty; her storehouse is without a door and completely depleted; her house is bare, and the locks off the chests lie about rusting underfoot.

[1] A clay ledge about a foot in height and width, adjacent to the foundations of a peasant's home. It deflected rain and was often used as a sort of bench to sit on.

She did not want to wait in the house until the cossacks came. And that house of hers was so decrepit and dilapidated!

She sat on the *prizba*, recalling her entire past. As she rested her head against the wall, her grey hair glistened in the sun like a ring from the top of a shiny plow. Her black eyes seemed to be lifting her forehead upward. It wrinkled and fled beneath her tight-fitting hair net from those large, sad eyes which explored the very depths of her soul to find there the treasures of her whole life.

Far away, at the foot of the mountains, the cannons roared, villages were in flames, and black smoke stretched itself like a dragon across the blue sky, seeking crevices in that azure depth, so that somewhere in them it might wash the blood and grime off itself.

Behind her shoulders the windows rattled after every thunderous outburst of the cannons. Perhaps her sons were there; perhaps they were already wrapped in the snow's white mantle, blood gushing out of them and painting crimson flowers upon it.

She brought them into the world strong and healthy, like wood-blocks. The bigger she became, the harder she worked, and after she bore each one of them, she appeared even more beautiful and cheerful than before. As for milk, she had so much of it that she could not only nurse them but bathe them in it. Her husband was strong and loving, and she had wealth besides.

At times, she and her husband would cut grain in the field all night, lulling their children into dreamland with the ringing sound of their sickles. And when the little ones slept covered behind them what more did she need, or what had she to fear? Unless it was that a star might fall on the children's heads. But she was so lively that she could have caught even a star on the point of her sickle.

And when they had harvested a measure of sixty sheaves, they would rest. Her young husband would start kissing her, and her joyful laughter drove away the birds from their nightly lodging. Not until their shadows reached the limits of the cultivated fields, and the moon was already setting, did they lie down beside their children. And in the morning the sun awakened them together with the children. She led them to a small well and rinsed the dew from their heads, and then the eldest boy would lug a pitcher of water to his father. The husband would remain in the field, and she would go home with the children, one in her arms and two at her apron strings. Along the road she played with them, like a girl with her ribbons. She caressed and fondled them. How could she begrudge them her time! She was strong and healthy, able to do everything quickly. All her children were growing up sound and hardy, not one of them was ever ailing. They went to school. Her feet never tiring, she followed them to all the towns, carrying loaves of plaited bread and white shirts for them on her back. Once, when they were jailed in Lviv[2] for rioting,[3] she took the train, and it seemed to speed and fly as fast to her sons as if her heart were burning in the engine up ahead. Among those well-born mothers for the first time in her life she felt equal to all the gentlefolk, and rejoiced that her sons had placed her on the same level with the gentry. And during vacation time her sons' friends came from all directions, and the house appeared to expand and become a mansion. They sang, carried on discussions, read books favourable to the common people. That was why people clung to them, blossomed in their presence, and prepared, by means of the young ones' knowledge, to regain the peasant rights which the lords had, from time immemorial, buried in their palaces. They marched in rows, carrying banners above them, and the gentry stepped aside to let them by.

And when the war began, the two older boys started to get ready for it immediately. Even the youngest one did not want to be left behind. All night long she prepared things for their journey, covering her mouth with her fist to stifle a cry that might awaken them. And when at daybreak, in the still starry dawn, she saw them sleeping so peacefully, she was herself at peace. She sat down near them, at their heads, and looked at them gently from the peep of day until sunrise. And in that short space of time her hair turned completely grey.

In the morning, when her husband saw her, he said:

"Your head has educated them. Let it now remain grey."

Later, she accompanied them to the city. At every step she kept hoping that one of the older boys would turn around to her and say:

"Mother, we are leaving you the youngest one to help and comfort you."

2 Capital of the province of Galicia, Western Ukraine.

3 Ukrainian students often demonstrated against the discriminatory Polish policies designed to suppress the development of Ukrainian cultural, political and economic life.

But not one of them turned, not one of them spoke those words. The grey stubbly hairs at her temples communicated their own whispers into her soul, murmuring into her ears:

"Indeed, they have forsaken you. Your genteel sons have forgotten their peasant mother."

A bitter droplet seeped out of her heart and poisoned her instantly.

The city teemed with young men, sons of the gentry and peasant boys.

Flags and banners rustled above them, and songs about Ukraine resounded.

Along the stone buildings mothers were holding their hearts in the palms of their hands and blowing on them to ease their pain.

When the sun was setting, all three of them came to her. They came to bid her farewell.

She led them a short distance away from the crowds.

Taking a knife out of her sleeve, she said: "Let Dmitro, the youngest, stay behind, or I'll plunge this knife into me." She said that and at once realized that with that knife she had cut the world in two: on one side she was left all alone, and on the other – her sons who were departing far from her. . . . And she fainted.

She regained consciousness when the earth rumbled beneath the long columns of the Sitch[4] troops who were singing their military song.

Dmitro was standing beside her.

"Let's run after them, my dear son, I want to catch up with them and ask them to forgive me, a stupid woman that I am. I didn't really understand. I'm innocent. I lost my mind when I saw this Ukraine taking my children from me. . . ."

She ran, and called: "Ivan! Andriy!" All the mothers there were running behind those long even columns of their sons, falling on their knees and lamenting.

---

[4] The Ukrainian Sitch Sharpshooters. The name "Sitch" was adopted by the Ukrainian volunteers who warred against the Polish and Russian troops in defense of their land. It was derived from the appellation taken by the first Cossack military establishment on the banks and islands of the lower Dnieper in the sixteenth century, particularly on the island of Khortitsia. It is thought that 'Sitch' was derived from the verb 'sikty' – to slash or cut with a sword or any sharp weapon.

Maria roused herself from her drowsiness and past memories, wrung her hands and cried:

"My children, my sons, where are your white bones? I will go, gather them up and bring them home on my back."

She felt that she had long been left alone in the world. Glancing at the sky, she became aware that under that blue lid she sat in utter loneliness, and that never again would her sons return to her, because the whole world had gone mad – man and beast.

Everything alive had been fleeing. Only recently all the roads were overcrowded. Children carried still younger ones than themselves; behind them their mothers were burdened with bundles full of their belongings; and in the general press, many involuntarily pushed others into precipices. At night the cows lowed, the sheep bleated, and the horses trampled on people and on one another.

Behind these demented people the world was aflame, as if to light their way to hell. All were leaping into a river glittering with the scarlet redness of the sky and resembling an avenging sword stretching across the earth. The roads sounded dully and creaked; their speech was frightening, as were the shrieks born of that mad rage when stone and steel devouringly ground against each other. It seemed as if the earth were complaining about the wounds inflicted on her.

And when the cannons met along the river bank, they heaved the earth out of its primeval bed. Houses rocketed up like flaming bales; people sunk into the earth were petrified with fear and unable to raise their arms to make the sign of the cross over their children; the crimson river formed a foam from the blood, and, like a wreath, its ferment revolved near the heads of corpses that floated gently down the stream.

After the battle, graves were dug and the dead were dragged out of the water.

In a few days the field gave birth to many, many crosses. And between those crosses the soldiers led away her youngest son, because he called the Tsar an executioner. They said that he was being taken to Siberia. A long way to go. Blood would drip from his boyish feet, leaving red traces behind him. . . . And her old husband, too, had driven some officers past those little crosses and disappeared to this day.

"O you pitiful creatures, you have left me alone with the owls to watch over your deserted hovels!"

* * *

Just at the moment when Maria's recollections, full of grief and despair, were weaving a sheet to hide from before her eyes that abyss in her past life, the cossacks entered the yard through the gate.

She was angry, because they never allowed her to remain in peace, and spoke to them in a loud voice:

"Ah, here you come again, you robbers!"

"Mother, we'll not rob you of anything. We just want to warm ourselves in your house. Let us in. The soul is just about frozen in the body."

She answered:

"Then go and warm yourselves in the cold house."

"And what about you?"

"You can beat me right now with your knouts, but for a mistress, as you see, I'm too old."

One of the cossacks – he was quite young – approached her and asked her quite earnestly to enter the house with them, for they would not go in alone.

"We are your people," he said, "we are not Russians or Turks."

"And just because you're ours, you go and tear our flesh with knouts, and others take and hang our people. The dead swinging from the trees in the woods are such a frightful sight that even wild beasts run away. . . ."

The youthful cossack pleaded with her so long and kindly that at last she entered the house with them.

She stood at the threshold while they seated themselves at the table.

"Sell us something to eat. We're hungry, mother."

"What will I give you to eat? There's some bread on the shelf up there. As for money, I don't want it. Some of you give it while others come around and take it away, and flog us besides. Your Tsar[5] is so great and rich, and yet he sends you to war without bread? Stand on the bench and reach for a loaf on the shelf."

Along with the bread he pulled out of the shelf a picture of Shevchenko[6] which had been turned with its face to the wall.

"Take the bread but give me back the picture. It belongs to my sons. Once, cossacks such as you took it from under the holy pictures, threw it on the ground and told me to trample on it. I hid it in my bosom, and they slashed my flesh with whips so hard that I don't even remember when they left the house."

[5] Nicholas II.

[6] The greatest Ukrainian poet, Taras Shevchenko.

She snatched Shevchenko's picture from the cossack's hands and put it inside the front part of her shirt.

"You may slaughter me right here but I will not give you the picture."

The youthful cossack, who had so gently begged her to enter the house with them, approached her, kissed her hand, and said:

"Dearest mother, I've spent a long time in prison for celebrating Shevchenko's anniversary. Wouldn't you give us the picture so that we can restore its honour and place it back under the holy pictures?"

"Who are you anyway? What kind of people are you? Where do you come from? You allow Jews to keep their faith and their writings, but you destroy all that is ours. The snow has now covered the roads, but, if it wasn't for that, you'd see the books from our libraries scattered all over them, throughout whole villages. All that the poor people had acquired for the education of their children – all that has gone under the horses' hoofs."

"Please, do give us the picture."

Slowly she pulled it out and handed it to him, for she herself was curious to see what they would do with it.

They placed two loaves of bread, one on top of the other, leaned the painting against them, pulled out embroidered and crocheted kerchiefs, and adorned the picture with them.

"Only ask yourselves, cossacks, whether it will be pleasant for this picture when you decorate it with Jewish cloth you got by robbery."

At that moment, one of the cossacks, who was already grey-haired, sprang to his feet and removed his cape. He was without a shirt.

"Let this, dear mother, tell you all about our robbing. All of us are going about without shirts, though we could have come by many of them. All these kerchiefs, with which we have adorned Shevchenko, are our cossack silken cloths, dear mother. They were given to us by our wives, mothers, sisters – to cover our heads with when we die on the battlefield, so that ravens wouldn't pluck out our eyes."

Maria glanced at them, came forward hesitantly, and said:

"No doubt, you are those whom my sons loved . . . Ukrainians. . . ."

"We are. And we're slaughtering each other."[7]

[7] Ukrainians under Russia, as well as those under Austria fought on opposite sides.

Maria climbed up to the shelves,[8] took out a shirt from the chest and handed it to one who was partly undressed.

"Put this on. It is my son's. God knows whether he will ever return to wear it."

The cossack took the shirt and timidly put it on.

"Let's not waste any time, cossacks. Let's pay our respects to Shevchenko, our Sire. We can eat the bread when we're on our way. You know how far we have to ride yet," said the commander of the cossacks.

They began to sing.

The windows started to vibrate, and the song, weaving itself into the sunbeams, escaped through the glass and winged its way into the village.

The women heard it and gathered at the gate, slowly moved to the window and finally, somewhat shyly, entered the porch and then the house itself.

"Maria, what's going on at your place? Are they drunk or just luring the girls with songs?"

"No, they are others, different ones."

"What others?"

"They are others because they are ours. Keep quiet and listen!"

Maria opened her eyes wide at the cossacks, then stepped forward, as if wanting to rush ahead and prevent their song from escaping out of the house.

The song was restoring her soul.

Somewhere in the sky, it revealed her whole life, all the stars that she had seen since childhood, all the dew that had ever fallen upon her head, all the gentle breezes that had ever caressed her face.

That song drew from her depths, as from some long-forgotten treasure chest, all that was enchanting and bright, and unfolded it before her. She could not see enough of herself in that wonderful new dawn.

Somewhere on the distant mountain top an eagle is perched. That song unfurls his wings, and the wafting of those wings brings a healing breeze to her heart, cleansing it of the black blood.

She feels the grip of her sons' little hands as they hold onto her sleeves, and sees them grow with every strain of the song. She hears every word of theirs that was ever spoken, and every discourse about Ukraine. All the indistinct and secret names are be-

---

8 Many peasant homes had a narrow row of shelves covered with beautifully woven rugs.

ing woven from the raying tresses of the stars and, like strings of a precious necklace, are twined around her neck.

The rivers glitter all across our land and thunderously fall into the sea, while the whole nation springs to its feet. Her sons are in the lead, and, together with them, she is marching to Ukraine, for it is she, that Ukraine of theirs, that weeps for her own children and desires them all to be united.

That lamentation cries its way to Heaven. Its canopy wrinkles and tears itself apart, while the song stops at the threshold and, before God, delivers its complaint. . . .

When they stopped singing, Maria stood motionless, as though she were a picture painted on canvas.

From a group of women, who had gathered in great number, one who was quite old approached the table.

"So you are ours! Thank God that you have come at last," she said.

"O, my poor dears, no one likes us. How many soldiers have passed through here, and none liked us. And how many people they have depraved and plundered! No matter where it was, whether in a city, or on the road, or even in our own village, we were foreigners, And no one would believe us."

"And what on earth do you expect of them? They're not our soldiers. They are the same as those about whom books were written, or such as were painted in pictures, when they were still ours.[9] But now they are Muscovites. How are they able to help us now? Perhaps on the quiet, when there's no one around to hear them, they might talk."

"You are young and able to read, so you know better. And I thought they were ours."

"Don't even say that, because we could be severely punished for it."

The old woman quickly mingled with the group of women who looked on with intense longing and breathed with despair.

On the other hand, young Katerina moved forward and stood at the very edge of the table.

"Look at Maria, in whose house we are gathered, look how petrified she's become by your song. She mourns for her sons. Two

---

[9] "Ours" means "our own," i.e., Ukrainian, such as were the cossacks who warred against the enemies of Ukraine in previous centuries. Under the sway of Russia, many Ukrainians, especially those who served in the tsarist army, became partly Russified and were no longer "ours," although quite a number of them still retained the memory of their national origin.

of them joined our volunteers, and the youngest one was taken by the Muscovites to Siberia. It seems that he had been among cossacks like you and had railed at the Tsar for persecuting our people so much. They immediately nabbed him, and he just disappeared. They were all well educated; much wealth had gone into their schooling. In the whole village no other mother grieves as much for her sons."

"Poor, unfortunate Maria!" whispered the women.

"It was something like this when, before the war, we were piling up a mound for this Shevchenko that's on the table before you. Other villages were heaping up mounds in his memory, so did we. There was so much trouble about it! The oldsters would not allow this mound-piling during the day, because there was work to be done in the fields. So we plotted together and did the piling at night; some with horses, others with wheelbarrows, and still others with spades. At last we had a mound heaped up as high as a bell-tower. Maria and her three sons also helped."

"Yes, but what good came from all that heaping? It only caused trouble for the village. The Muscovites came, dug up the mound, scattered it about and trampled all over it. They seemed to have been searching for money or something. And because of that mound my Mikhaylo disappeared."

"Even if your Mikhaylo has disappeared for good, the people will never forget him. He wasn't afraid of the Muscovites, and told them the truth."

"'Like pigs,' he said, 'you have rooted up the whole of Ukraine, and now you've come here, to us, to do more rooting?'"

"It's all very well for you, Katerina, to talk, but he left behind a wife and children."

"Mine, too, left me behind with children."

"At least one of you must be educated. Why not write something so that the whole world will know how the Muscovites are liberating us from the yoke. We won't soon forgive them for dishonouring that mound. It was already dawning, and the dew had covered us when we finished that mound. We sat down, because our feet were aching. Then Maria's older son climbed to the very top and spoke to us so beautifully, saying that from this our mound we would be able to look up to that great mound in Ukraine, and that we all should be of one mind. He gazed ahead with such wonder as though, in reality, he was seeing Ukraine, there among the stars. Then we got up and sang such songs as you are singing now."

At this moment Katerina approached a cossack and whispered almost into his ear:

"Your songs are the same as those of Maria's sons. So don't awaken her. Let her go on imagining that it is her sons who are singing. . . ."

Children's Adventure

"Vasylko,[1] here's Nastia.[2] Take her to uncle's place, that way, down the path along the forest. You know how to get there. But hold her hand lightly, don't jerk her, because she's very small. And don't carry her either, because you're not strong enough."

She sat down but, feeling great pain, she lay down on the ground.

"How should I know which way to take her at night? You go ahead and die, and we'll be beside you. I'll take her there in the morning."

"You see, Nastia? The bullet just swished and killed mother. And you're to blame. Why did you bawl when that soldier wanted to put his arms around mother? Why should that have bothered you? We were running away, and the bullet whistled. . . . And now you won't have a mother. You'll have to go to work for a living. . . .

"She's not talking anymore; she's dead already. I could give you a good beating, but you're an orphan now. Besides, what's a girl like you worth? When Ivan's wife, who lived near us, died, her girls never stopped lamenting: 'Mother, dear mother, where are we to look for you, where will we find you again?'. . . But you don't know how to lament. And I'm a boy. It's not proper for boys to lament.

"Do you see the soldiers on the other side flash their lights this way, like water through a sieve? As soon as the beam flashes, they see where the soldier on this side is. A bullet hits him, and he

[1] Diminutive of Vasyl, Basil.
[2] Colloquial for Anasthasia.

tumbles down, just like mother. Quickly, lie down beside mother, because the bullets will soon be flying. Do you hear them go bang-bang?

"Just look at the soldiers on the other side of the Dniester[3] throw up those flaming bullets. They hurl them high, so very high. The bullet burns and then its light goes out. They're just playing with them, with so many of them. . . .

"And listen to the cannon say boom, boom! But it doesn't shoot at people, only at churches, houses and schools.

"Never be afraid of the cannon. The bullet in it is just as big as me, and its wheels are as large as those of windmills. Ah, you don't know anything yet; you can't even walk right, but I'm big and can romp about like a horse. . . .

"Hide yourself behind mother. Look, they're flashing again, and the light is white, as white as a sheet. They'll soon turn the lights on us. . . . Look how white we are, and the bullets are already whistling above us. So what! If a bullet hits me, I'll lie down beside mother and die, and then you wouldn't get to uncle's place yourself. It would be better if the bullet killed you first. I could get to the uncle myself and let him know where to find you so he could bury you both.

"Already you're crying as if a bullet hit you. All it does is swish and bore a hole in you, and your soul flies out of you through that hole, and then you're gone. It's not like home where they rub you with whiskey when you get sick. . . .

"So you're crying because you're hungry . . . well, glory be! What am I going to give you to eat when mother is dead? Let mother give it to you. Tell mother, go ahead, tell her. Well, does she answer? Go and take her by the hand, take it. You see, the hand falls down. Didn't I tell you? What a foolish girl you are! Mother's soul has gone out of her, and now it's that soul that speaks, gives bread, and even beats you. . . .

"For goodness sake, Nastia, I'll sure give you a beating. What on earth am I going to give you to eat? Just keep on looking at the war and see how nice it is. And tomorrow we'll go to uncle's place and eat borshch. Now, just a minute. I think mother has some bread inside the breast of her shirt. . . . Hush! Mother does have some there. Here, eat, you greedy girl.

"Again they're spreading the sheet, and what a white one, as white as snow. It's coming down on us. O! Nastia, what's happened to you? My goodness, all your mouth is bloody, and the

[3] A river in the southern part of Western Ukraine.

hands too. Did a bullet hit you? My poor, poor Nastia, lie down beside mother . . . what else can you do?

"Oh, it's not a bullet that hit you, it's the bread that got soaked in the blood inside mother's shirt. What a bad girl! She eats like a pig, and just look at how she smeared her face and hands with blood. . . . How am I to take you to the village to-morrow so smudged with blood? But don't worry. When I'll be taking you along the brook, I'll wash it off you, but in such cold water that you'll holler at the top of your voice. And I'll beat you if you do.

"Have you had enough? Then lie down beside mother, and I'll lie down next to you. Don't be scared, the wolf won't eat you up, because you'll be in the middle. You go to sleep, and I'll still look at the war. Move closer and warm yourself against me. . . .

"Maybe a bullet has already killed daddy in this war, and before morning it'll kill me and Nastia? Then there'll be nobody, nobody. . . ."

He fell asleep. Till the day grew light, the white bright cover trembled above them and continually moved rapidly beyond the Dniester.

C. H. A.

The Baby-Watcher

Parasia,[1] a small baby-watcher, sits and holds a child in her lap. Around her there are many such watchers, boys and girls. The entire group appears like oversized wild apples which someone had shaken down from the tree and just let lie on the ground, in the dust.

Parasia suggests that they play funeral and lament.

"Why funeral? And why lament?"

"I'll tell you why. During the night I heard my father say that this child should not be in the house, because it's not our baby. It belongs to the Russian hussar. So my father said to my mother:

---

[1] Colloquial for Paraskeva.

'Either kill it or bury it, I don't want it.' And mother said: 'How can I bury a live child?' – 'Then kill it and bury it after.' That's why I've been waiting with this child for you, while you were still asleep, because father shouted: 'Get out of here with this bastard!' "

Little Maksim, who was always much taken up with the hussars, let the child he was holding on his lap slip to the ground and carefully began to examine the hussar's baby.

He said:

"This child is like any other. Your father must be crazy."

"But what if my father wants to choke this baby?"

"Well, there's no trick to choking a small thing like that. If he chokes it, they'll bury it."

"And what a lament your mother will raise! Ah-h-h!"

"Let's start a lament, but only the girls. The boys must be quiet, because they're not supposed to lament."

The small girls started to wail, imitating women, and the entire village common was filled with a funereal sound.

From behind the gate Dmitro's[2] old wife shouted to them:

"What are you doing? Have you lost your senses to begin lamenting so loud? It's a sin to lament when there's no one dead."

"Old woman, this is the hussar's baby, and it must die. They'll have to choke it to death, and that's why it's not a sin to lament."

The old woman crossed herself, and the children continued their lamentation.

C.H.A.

The Sons

Old Maksim[1] was harrowing his spring-field with a good team of young horses. The harrows flew over the field like feathers. Maksim threw his hat far out on the plowed land. His shirt came unbuttoned and slipped from his shoulders down to his back. A

2 Colloquial for Demetrius.
1 Maximius or Maximian.

cloud of dust from under the harrows covered the grey hair on his head and chest. He shouted, raged, and the people in the neighboring fields were saying to themselves:

"The old dog is always furious, but he still holds the young horses firmly. He is rich, and was well fed in his youth, but he lost both his sons, and ever since he's always fuming in the field as well as in the village."

Maksim reined in his horses.

"Old bones are like old willows; they're good for firewood but are useless in keeping up with horses. When legs wobble behind the horses and fail you in a dance, then I'd better not say what such legs are worth. Better crawl up onto the top of the clay-stove, grandpa, because your time is come."

He shook his hoary head under the horses' black manes and continued shouting:

"I still can crawl up onto the top of the stove, but it's cold and peeled all over up there. The holy pictures on the walls have turned black, and the saints are looking at the empty house like hungry dogs. All her life my old woman garlanded them with periwinkle and sweet basil, and gilded the doves in front of them so that they would be kind to us, that the house would be bright, that the children would grow. But though they are many, all those saints are good for nothing. The sons are gone, the old wife I've burrowed into the ground, so you, gods, must excuse the absence of the periwinkle. You should have taken better care. . . . Well, Starface, for as long as God has appointed us time to work, let's tackle this land."

And they trudged from one end of the field to the other, wrapped in a cloud of dust, while the harrows were snarling and biting into the soil, crumbling it in order to make a soft bed for the seed.

"You, Bossak, you're no horse at all, you're a dog. You've chewed up both my shoulders. There's mark upon mark all over them from your bites. At least don't you tug at me, because life has been tugging me so hard that I can hardly stand on my feet. At dawn I feed you oats, even before I've eaten myself; I brush you clean, I wet you with my old tears, and you're biting me? To me, Starface is quite a man;[2] he follows me with his black eyes; he pities me; he wipes grandpa's tears with his mane, but you're a bad one, a heartless beast. Just the other day you snatched out a tuft of my hair and let it fall underfoot, into the manure. You

2 Maksim is so attached to this horse that he as much as considers him human.

shouldn't do that. For even if you are a very fine horse, still you are bad. I can't sell you to Jews, but if St. George ever came to me, by God! I'd make you a gift to him so that you might go killing the dragons with him. You're not fit to work the land with, because there's no steadiness in you."

Wetting his fingers with saliva, he kept washing the wound on his back shoulder and covering it with dust.

"Hey, horses, let's go, let's go!"

The harrows were quieting down, the soil was giving in and becoming pulverized. Maksim felt softness underfoot, such softness as very seldom visits a muzhik's soul. It is the soil that gives him that softness, and that is why he loves it so much. And as he cast handfuls of seed, he kept saying; "I've made a soft cradle for you. May you grow 'way up to heaven."

Maksim was becoming calmer. He was not shouting any more. Suddenly, he halted his horses.

"Why the devil do you smart, creaking in every joint, you old crooked bone?"

He glanced backward and, seeing a long streak of blood alongside the harrow, sat down.

"Glass got into my foot, damn it! Now go ahead and harrow. You'll have to, because you won't leave the field unfinished, unless you split yourself into pieces. And you, my poor land, will gain little from this old blood, because old blood, like old manure, yields nothing. To me it's a loss, and no gain to you."

Limping, he unharnessed the horses, led them to the wagon and placed some hay in front of them.

"You, Sun, don't frown at the old man for calling dinner too early. The old man has nothing to walk with."

From a bag he pulled out bread, salted pork and a bottle, and washed his wound with whiskey. Then he tore off a piece of his shirt sleeve, wrapped it around his foot and tied it with a cord from the bag.

"Now either keep hurting or stop, or do whatever you like, but you're going to harrow."

He had a drink of whiskey, took the bread and, biting into it, became angry again and resumed his shouting:

"Is this bread? It's only fit to curry a Jew's horse with, because it would tear the hide off a good horse. . . . Those worn-out hags are swarming around me: 'Grandpa,' they say, 'we'll bake for you, we'll wash for you, but deed some of your land to us.' Those bedraggled bitches think that I kept the land for them! After I die,

144

let little flowers grow on my land and with their tiny heads let them say the Lord's Prayer for grandpa."

Angrily, he flung the bread far out on the plowed field.

"This linseed grub is making my teeth gnash. Drink whiskey, my dear Maksim. It goes down smoothly.

"Hey you, shut up there. Don't squawk over my head. For who did you burst into song, anyway? For this ragged and gnawed old man? Better fly to heaven and tell your God not to send me a silly bird with a song. For if He is so powerful, let Him send me my sons, because it's by His will that I'm left alone on this whole earth. Let not your God fool me with songs. Away with you!"

He hurled a lump of earth at the skylark, but the bird continued to sing even more beautifully and refused to fly to God.

"You're a dumb bird. You understand nothing, nothing at all. When my little Ivan chased after you, hoping to catch you, when he hunted for your nest along the boundary lines, and played the flute, then, birdie, you were wise to sing your song; it was the right thing to do. Your song and Ivan's flute flowed down below and, with the sun above you, all you birds poured out God's voice over my head, over the shiny plows, and over the happy world. And through the sun, as if through a golden sieve, God strewed brightness all over us, and all the people radiated gold. So did the sun leaven the spring on earth, as if in some huge trough. . . .

"And out of that trough we took out loaves of plaited bread, and all those plaited loaves stood in front of the musicians. Then was the time when our young ones, bedecked with flowers, and full of love, went to the altar, while the spring rolled along like a tidal wave, like a deluge. Then, my birdie, your song flowed into my heart like bracing water into a new pitcher. . . .

"Go away, little bird, go to those lands where they have not yet taken away the loaves of plaited bread, where the children haven't yet been slaughtered."

With both hands he grasped his hoary head and bent toward the earth.

"Shame on you, grey hairs, shame on you for prattling and trolling like a whining woman, because nothing in this world will ever help you. . . .

"O, my sons, my sons, where have your heads been laid? Not only my entire land but my very soul I'd sell to be able to walk with my bleeding feet to your graves. Lord! The golden books in the churches lie that You had a son, they lie that You had one! You've resurrected Yours, they say. But I'm not asking You to resurrect mine. All I'm asking You is to show me their graves, that I may lie beside them. You see the whole world, but over my sons' graves You've become blind. . . .

"May this blue dome of Yours crack into pieces, like my heart!

"Come. At least one of you come to see the old man. Haven't you embraced my sons and lain with them in white beds? My sons were like curly oaks. . . . Come, and bring the tiny bastard in your arms. Don't be ashamed, come. Grandpa will lay out all the best carpets under your feet and will cut up the finest linen into diapers for the bastard. Because you're walking about unwed and weeping for being scorned."

And the old man raised both his hands aloft and called, gesturing with them to the entire world:

"Come, daughter-in-law, come to daddy. We don't need a priest to tell us what to do."

He burst out into loud sobbing, lay down on the ground, wiped his tears off with the earth as with a handkerchief, blackening his face with it. And he pleaded further:

"Or you, who was the lover of one of them, come, even without a child. Come, and on your neck I'll see his arms, and his lips I'll see redden on yours. Out of your eyes, like out of a deep well, I'll catch his eyes and hide them in my heart, as in a case. Like a dog, I'll smell his hair on the palm of your hand. . . . Sweetheart, come and save the old man!

"You're still in this world, but they're not. So find a way to me and bring me some news of them. Pour down cold dew on my grey hair, because each one of them is burning like hot wire. The fire is scorching my head."

And he began tearing out his grey hair and tossing it to the ground.

"Scorch the earth, grey hairs; you're too heavy a burden for me!"

Exhausted to the limit, he slipped gently to the ground, remained silent for a long while, and then began to relate softly:

"I remember the last time Andriy[3] came to me. He was my educated one. 'Father,' said he, 'now we're going to fight for Ukraine.' – 'For what Ukraine?' – And he lifted a lump of earth with his sword and said: 'This is Ukraine, and here' – pointing the sword to his chest – 'here's her blood. We're going to take our land from the enemy. Give me a white shirt,' he said, 'give me some clean water to wash myself, and – farewell!' – When that sword of his flashed, it blinded me. 'Son,' I said, 'I've got one younger than you, Ivan. Take him along with you in this affair.

[3] Andrew.

146

He's strong enough. Then let me bury you both in our soil so that the enemy may not wrench it out for himself from these strong roots.' – 'Very well, father,' he said, 'both of us will go.' The moment my old woman heard this, I saw right then that death had wrapped itself around her like a white sheet. I made for the door, because I heard her eyes fall out and roll away on the ground like lifeless pieces of stone. So it seemed to me, but it was certain that the light on her forehead had already gone out. . . .

"In the morning, when both were leaving, my old wife leaned on the gate, but did not speak. She had a faraway gaze, as if she was looking from heaven itself. And when I took them to the train, I said: 'Andriy, Ivan, don't go back; and remember me, because I'm now alone. Your mother died at the gate. . . ."

Until nightfall Maksim steered his horses over the field and did not rave any more. He calmed down completely. Children who drove their sheep, and people who passed him by with their clattering plows, were afraid to greet him. Smeared with mud, ragged and limping, he looked as if he were sinking into the ground.

* * *

Late at night, after Maksim had tended the cows and horses, and milked the sheep, he entered the house.

"You, poor old thing, have become completely silent, lifeless, as if someone had stuck a knife into you. You can't utter a word. . . . But I'll stir up some fire in you yet. . . ."

He cooked some cornmeal, put on a white shirt, ate his supper and became quiet. Then he knelt on the earthen floor and prayed:

"And you, Mother of God, be my housekeeper. You with your son in the middle and Andriy and Ivan beside you both, on either side. . . . You gave one son, and I gave two."

Grandpa Hritz

I drove out to visit my old friend Hritz.[1] Deaf for quite a while now, he was hard to chat with. He was holding a green branch in his hands, and beside him on the grass sat his small grandson.

[1] Colloquial for Hrihoriy, Gregory.

"You've arrived at the right time. I feel transformed into a youngster. Only I don't know yet whether I'll turn into a mere child or bring shame down on my old head. I seem to hear the music that sounded loud and clear when my old woman and I were getting married, and whose din sharply filled my ears. Until now I felt as if they had been plugged with lead. It's really a torture to be deaf; the words wither on my tongue, while my old mate mocks me and screeches right into my ears like a jay. No more listening to what's going on at public meetings, or making speeches from the rostrums for me. I'm so lonesome for the sound of a human voice that I could almost have myself walled up and suffocate. It's so bitter to feel the still living body being crusted over as if with bark and become like a rugged post.

"There's nothing left for me to do but remain within my own soul and live there as in a sunken-in house where everything is shattered and laid waste. It's just like dragging your broken treasures out of a fog, out of wet ashes, and wiping the grime off your hands. My own children are like strangers. I have almost forgotten that at one time they were young."

* * *

"A very long time ago quite a number of us *hospodars*[2] from the Cheremosh[3] region and from beyond the Dniester[3] and the Prut[3] met in the city where we brought our sons to school. In the market place they were as silent as fish scattered along the road. They were just dying to make off for the green fields. The mothers sat in the wagons, weeping and in a low voice cursing those who advised us to do so. But we, the fathers, were delighted. 'How long,' we asked, 'will we be so foolish as to slave for our wealthy masters? When our children are educated, we'll drive the rich ones out.' And somewhat later, when our children did grow up and gained knowledge in school, we, the sturdy *hospodars*, swarmed and hummed around them like bees among flowers.

"That sad event, when I seemed to have fallen into a deep vault, cemented all around, caused me such sorrow that I began to forget all that I had ever enjoyed in life. But when several days ago I felt a new strength within me, then, O Lord! it was as though the entire Sun, which I had been carrying on my back like a burden for three generations, became light and enlivened me, and all the wheat that I had ever threshed was still there unthreshed. Now I am rich, rich enough to feed the entire

[2] Well-to-do peasants.

[3] Names of three rivers in the southern part of Western Ukraine.

Ukraine. All the frosts that I have been feeling so keenly beneath me are putting me back on my feet.

"I imagine myself going to visit my children once again. The old woman has filled the bag with all kinds of things. This for them, and that for them, but no pity for me as she loads me up as if I were a horse. I trudge through snowdrifts and battle a blizzard, happy in the thought that my children's welcome is ahead of me, and behind me stands my white cosy cottage awaiting my return.

"I wonder if they are growing healthy and sound, and if they are studying well.

"I relax along the way, feeling like a deep-rooted oak tree whose branches almost reach the sky and are to be found in the school where my children are. The pause has revived me, and I feel strong enough to do the rest of the walking down that road, because my chest is expanding with a kind and tender emotion."

* * *

"You should have seen the day when those children of ours finished school and came back. How they clung to us, and how tightly we pressed them as we surrounded them! Man! Who'd be scared of the gendarme restraining us now? Along with our children we forge ahead in thousands, strong and enlightened. Our own are in the lead. His forehead as bright as the sun, Franko[4] rises and in soft words teaches us, because he knows everything. He tells us that when every one of us serves a jail term for the muzhik's cause, none will ever know the meaning of fear. And Pavlyk,[5] all out of breath, in a determined high-pitched voice, as if completely without hope, relates our misery. And there, from the rear door, noisy Trilovsky,[5] in ribbons like a girl, shouts condemnations; while our young ones, for that very reason, press closer and closer to him. In a word, in the towns, the earth rumbled under our feet, and more than one corner timber in a rich man's house was loosened.[6]"

* * *

"And when Franko came to our house with a number of young people to stop for the night, my wife, though she did not like speeches, did not nag me in our small home, because she saw that

[4] The greatest poet and political writer in Western Ukraine, second only to Taras Shevchenko in importance.

[5] Mikhaylo Pavlyk, Kirilo Trilovsky, Ukrainian writers and political leaders.

[6] An impressionistic expression, implying the fear which the well-to-do felt in their homes when the poor reacted against the wrongs done to them.

our educated young people were bright and happy in his presence, as if he had placed a golden halo on each one's head. And I leaned against an ash tree in the garden and said: 'Lord! You have gladdened the world with all those stars, and us, poor muzhiks, with Franko. For him I will offer You a prayer every day!"

* * *

"Back in the house, I said to him: 'I have no schooling, but my boys read your books to me, the old ones and the new, one after another. If God would only give you enough strength to bring out of hiding all our writings, those in the earth, in old monasteries, and in palace vaults! And do remember us from time to time.' Next day I was driving Franko to the railway station and met some nobleman with horses that looked like dragons. But I didn't turn off the road, nor did I doff my hat to him. I thought to myself: 'You miserable noble! Beside me rides a much greater one than you!' "

* * *

"We increased in strength, our children multiplied, and we were all of the same spirit. The war took its toll and laid many a one in the damp earth. But those who survived, the ones whom we had reared, and whom Franko had taught, formed themselves into a single Ukrainian command. And that command spoke out: 'Ukraine must exist!' He who did not see those times here was certainly deprived of God's grace.

"The grandsons went away to the front, and I sent even my granddaughter to look after the sick and wounded in hospitals. Not one of them returned! My old woman raved like mad, damned me, and cursed Ukraine. 'You spent all your days listening to speeches,' she said, 'until the children caught the contagion and went headlong to their doom.' My children apparently said nothing, but they shunned me as one who had scattered the bones of their children all over the earth.

"I made up my mind to go and search for my grandchildren, but the Poles caught me at the border and dragged me back home. For many long years I lived behind the corners of my house and dared not enter it even for my meals. I made myself a bed in the stable among the cattle and lodged there summer and winter. I became deaf, almost blind, ate hardly anything. All I had was some potatoes and a little drink of water. I was forgotten by my children and the world. But the worst were our own people, those who went into government service.

"When the Polish gendarme comes and orders one of my sons to do compulsory transport duty, it is I who pick up the whip and drive away, as long as I know where to go.

" 'Well, old man,' I was teased, 'where is your Ukraine now? How many morgs[7] of land did you say you wanted to get from the landlord? And what kind of cabinet minister was your grandson going to be?'

" 'I'm deaf,' I would say, 'I don't hear a thing.'

"I either take them and their lady friends for a drive, or clean the streets, and do that sort of state duty without pay. But those of our people who have gone into Polish civil service or some other government department appear to avoid me, as if they didn't recognize me. The poor wretches roam about like pups let out by their masters into the open field.

"But a young lady teacher did recognize me. Without weeping or lamenting, she said to me: 'Grandpa Hritz, what am I to do? My principal wants me to adopt his faith,'[8] –'Poor girl," said I, 'don't go to visit those who despise your faith. Live in your own home and eat dark bread.' "

* * *

"And now I have a great favour to ask of you. Now that I seem to be revived, my good health may remain for a long or a short time. But when I die, come here immediately, because I'm afraid that, once I'm gone, my children will strip the walls and cast the pictures of Shevchenko,[9] Franko, and those of all our other friends into the attic. 'They murdered our children, and we can't stand the sight of them,' they will say. So when I'm already in the coffin, ask my children, in the presence of those who will be there, whether they are going to take as good care of my pictures as I have, or whether they are going to turn them with their faces to the wall, just to curry favor with the officials and gendarmes. This little grandson of mine here, he'd pay due respect to my friends, but he's far from being able.

"But if my children refuse to respect my saints, buy a leather case, put the pictures inside it and place them on my chest. They say that leather does not decay for ages.

[7] About an acre.

[8] The principal, a Pole, apparently wanted to marry the teacher, a Greek Catholic, but would not, unless she turned Roman Catholic. Or maybe he wanted to dismiss her for preserving her faith. The Poles, being Roman Catholic, were preferred for all higher positions.

[9] The greatest Ukrainian poet, Taras Shevchenko.

"And I have still another favor to ask: I'm leaving a chunk of land to anyone you yourself will name, so that when the time comes to gather up the bones of our soldiers[10] into heaps, he is to rake up several shovelfuls for me. But they must be piled up high, because on those bones our land will blossom again! As to my funeral, everything has been arranged. My children won't have to provide a single nail."

The next day, very early, a messenger came from grandpa Hritz. He said that, after I had driven away, the old man told his grandson to play the flute, had a drink of milk, joked tartly with his wife, dressed himself in a long white shirt, lit a candle in his hands, laid himself down on the bed, and instantly died.

The Thread

The house is quiet and the windows are dark. There is barely enough light to illuminate the picture of the Mother of God and the distaff.

The husband, Semen,[1] appears to love his wife even in his sleep. Maria and Vasyl[2] are fast asleep beside him. Yurko,[3] the youngest, is in the cradle beside her. She is glad to love and be loved in return. The holy pictures on the walls look down.

The house is tidied up. Perhaps she should be sitting down to the distaff.

"My husband is young and strong. I will have more children.

"No matter how many I give birth to, he will feed them all.

"The thread is long, exceedingly long – endless! No one has ever reached the end of thread-making. They must be clothed, because God has given them to me to love. I want my husband to feel upon him the work of my fingers – all ten of them. Maria must be dressed up for Easter; and those boys of mine, too, will

[10] The Ukrainian Sitch Sharpshooters who fought the Poles. See "Maria."
[1] Colloquial for Simon or Simeon.
[2] Basil.
[3] Colloquial for Yuriy, George.

be tearing their clothes, knowing that their mother will sew more of them."

The husband sleeps like a stone. Maria has uncovered herself, and Yurko, in the cradle beside her, is restless. She covers them and lowers her breast to reach him.

Her eyes are on the distaff, and the thread is being spun evenly, continuously.

"And when I weave enough for them and bleach the cloth as white as paper, I'll embroider all their garments.

"And from the gate I will look for them, for my husband and my children. They are all mine, as they come toward me in the sunlight."

By midnight the eyes grow tired and weary and the fingers numb, but the thread must be spun on and on.

Her young body slowly inclines toward the distaff.

"I must not weaken. All those asleep are depending on me. I will spin my thread to the very end."

And the Mother of God came down from the holy pictures to help her.

But she did not assist her very long. One night she came and said:

"I will help you no longer. Come with me."

An Ancient Melody

My sister and I sat on top of the clay-stove[1] in our white, shirts. Mother, still quite young, awaited the coming of the carol-singers from the church Brotherhood. Her white hemstitched sleeves seemed glad to cover her strong youthful arms.

"Children, don't be naughty when the Brothers come. Do be quiet. You'll find honey cakes and sugar up there. You may have as much as you like, only behave yourselves."

In a little while we heard the creaking of big boots in the snow in front of the windows. A hurricane of an ancient melody

[1] See page 27.

burst from manly chests. The carol told of a knight and how his faithful steed reproached him:

"You will sell me and then grieve as you recall me."

The horse continued to remind the knight of the wars he had carried him through – those with the Polovetsians,[2] Turks, and Muscovites.

The refrain of Ukrainian history sounded heroically as recounted by that horse.

"Behind me cannons roared like thunder."

I became frightened of those cannons and hid in the corner. But out of sympathy for the steed I began to cry. And Maria said: "You're always silly!" For this she got a poke in the ribs from me and began to bawl.

Mother could hardly make us calm down.

The carol-singers came into the house. The loaves of plaited bread on the table were almost as large as they. They carolled for mother, and they carolled for Maria, while behind me, on top of the clay-stove, cannons roared like thunder. And I was dying to see that steed, for he must have been different from our horses which pull the plow.

"Brother Semen, we will now carol for your little boy."

"If you please, Brothers."

> *"Early, very early Vasyl[3] arose,*
> *By the first candle he washed his face,*
> *By the second he dressed himself apace,*
> *By the third he saddled his horse. . . ."*

It seemed to me that I was already in the saddle and firmly vowing never to sell my steed.

"Come down and thank the Brothers."

My father picked me up in his arms and I kissed everyone's hard, iron-like hand. In return, I received a kreutzer from each of the Brothers. And when the palm of my hand could not hold so many kreutzers, my mother took them from me and tied them in a red kerchief.

My lips swelled from so much kissing, but I kissed every last one of them. Then my father carried me back to the top of the clay-stove.

I fell asleep, very happy. The money the Brothers had given

2 A tribe roaming on the territory of Ukraine about a thousand years ago.
3 Basil.

me was soon spent, but the cannons behind me roar like thunder to this very day.

The Boundary Line

"Lord God, in the days of my youth You visited me with my sin less often, but now You don't depart from me for a single hour. But I'm telling You, I'm not sorry in the least."

"What are you saying, old man? Stop sinning."

"Get out of the house – all of you!"

They leave. The mother explains to the daughters that their father has reached the age of seventy, that he is very ill, that for the last ten years he has been speaking hardly above a whisper, but now he roars like thunder as he seeks to justify himself before God. The mother weeps and the daughters weep. Soon they quietly slip back into the house.

"Whether it's a sin or not, even now I'll not give up the land. Why, he's such a rich man, possesses such large tilled fields, and yet he comes to take away my portion of the soil. He wants to swallow up my field. I cultivate it so carefully, tending it on every side. Where there are thistles I bend down and weed them out. My back is cracking and my hands burn from the prickles. I'm not able to straighten out at nights or soothe my hands with my tongue as a dog does his wound."

His aged wife beside him crosses herself.

"In the spring my fields are green and whisper with the wind. And I lie down on the ground and thank the wind for being on earth, and the earth for making things grow. And their conversation gave birth to a prayer in me to You, such as You have never heard before. And for this prayer You should forgive me my sin."

"Oh, father, do not say such things."

"I'm talking to God. Get out of the house!"

Again they go out, and again they silently return.

"And when the earth falls asleep, exhausted like a mother who has fed her children and covered herself with white sheets, as a swan with its wings, I often felt it sinful to clear away the snow, because she might get cold and wake up. The earth is Your daughter, and for her sake You should forgive me."

As she weeps, his old wife is sorrowfully nodding her head.

"He insists on taking it away from me. But I put a scythe under my arm and plunge it into his very heart. 'Now go and have your fill of that earth.' I served my sentence. Well, what if I was imprisoned within stone walls? My longing for my soil did not become rusty. I returned and embraced my tilled fields. The rich people, however, shied away from me and kept their distance. And You, God, continued to visit me with Your punishment. I did not wrangle with You, but I tell You that I was right."

His wife and daughters raised a lament.

"Bitches, carry me outside, and yourselves remain in the house."

And the bitches did so.

"I am not to be compared to our people who directed bullets and cannons against the enemy because of their boundary line.[1] The young are like bubbling froth. They sing as they go to their death. But we who are left behind gather our own singers and weep. Those young people are caked in blood, black with mud, and rifles cannot be wrested from their dead hands. Only their eyes smile, because their mothers weren't there to close them. And I weep and think: 'For as long as we go on burying those smiling pearl-like eyes, that boundary line will be ours.' And why, God, did You not bless them?

"Since then, God, I have not been afraid of You."

"Oh, children, pray for your sinful father. He is dying."

"I will be in my death-throes soon. See that you cover me with earth in the coffin, and do not dress me. I want to be alone with the soil, like those who died on the battlefield. And You, God, if it is Your will, forgive me, and if not, then hurl me down into Your eternal prison. You do have a Hell. I will not take my complaints to anyone higher than You.

"Put me down on the earth that I may kiss it once more."

"Oh, my children, our father has already died in sin."

---

[1] Here the boundary line, by extension, means the boundary of the entire territory of Ukraine. The reference is to Ukrainian War of Independence with the Poles (1917-21) in which Ukraine lost her short-lived freedom.

Sin

Kassian's wife is simply wondering what will happen. Yesterday her husband returned from the front, had a drink of water, and is now fast asleep. He smells of the soot from the locomotive. An oil-lamp is flickering on top of the oven. Next to her, on one side, sleeps their child whom she bore before the war. With every turn the girl keeps on uncovering herself. And time and again the Russian bastard is seeking his mother's bosom. Her round breast is projected on the wall as large as a hillock, and there, too, the bastard's lips appear like those of a voracious dragon. Meanwhile she thinks: "This boy is like a vampire; he's drawn out all my womanly honour, and now he's going to drain all the blood out of me."

*   *   *

"What will happen when my husband gets up? I can just see him twist my long braids around his hands and drag my beautiful body, thumping it under the benches and against the stove pegs. Then he will pull me to the doorstep, knock my head against the corner of the porch and leave me there so that the dogs could lick the blood trickling from my pate. Such will be the penance for your sin, you bitch. And this poor infant of mine will be lost in dirt and scorn. No one will even give him a shirt to wear. And when, God forbid, he grows up without a name, like a waif, fit only to be a menial, he won't even hear about his father who, out on the broad plain, will not be aware of him at all. My God, why have You punished me so cruelly as to make me lose my reason when he looked into my lovely eyes and filled the inside of his army greatcoat's fronts with my braids? God, You are to blame, because You deprived me of my senses. You wink at me with your bright stars and laugh. Be just as accursed as I am!"

*   *   *

"For three days my mother stood at the doorpost, sad, her honour injured, while my sisters with their tears washed the diapers for my bastard. For weeks my father wouldn't enter the house, and ate his hard crust of bread outside. The priest in the church laid a curse on me, and people passed me by without a word. Even a hill of rock wouldn't be able to bear such a burden.

And the only reason I didn't throw myself into the Danube was my bastard who smiled at me with his silken eyes."

She seized her child, pressed it hard to herself, and went on:

"Who could give me force enough to go outside right now, sharpen a knife and plunge it into his very heart? O God! You make man prone to commit sin, but You don't give him the strength to wash the sin away. No, I won't kill you, poor wretch. Although I feel an urge in me to do so, my heart is trembling like a cobweb in the breeze. O, if I could only snatch my heart out and stuff it down your throat, so that you might die with two hearts and I without any!"

* * *

It was early in the morning.

"Whose child is this?"

"You should know it's not yours, but mine."

"Well, we'll bring this one up too."

"No, I don't want you to bring up my children. I'll bring them up myself."

With her steel-like hands she pressed the boy to herself. She thought he would bash her head with an axe. In fact, she preferred to perish first so as not to look at the last spasms of those tiny arms.

"Now I see, my husband. You're not a man, but a woman. So you're really not joking? Do you find it so easy to bear the shame of your wife?

"Do you know that ever since I've become a whore, all the rakes rap on my windows? I am no longer a wife to you. You don't need a wife like me.

"I am leaving Katerina with you. She's pretty big now, and she's yours. I am going away with my child."

Out of her hope chest she picked a few things of her trousseau. For herself she took two shirts and a small sheepskin jacket.

"What remains here," she said, "is for Katerina. She's very clever and polite. You'll be very happy with her."

She walked down the street with the child in her arms.

Her mother and father, her sisters and all the neighbours shouted after her:

"Don't go, don't go!"

But she was almost running.

When she reached the top of the hill and saw the cliffs of the high mountains and the shiny river, she sighed deeply, gave her son one of her breasts to suck, and whispered:

"Sin, O my sin! I will make up for what I have done. And in my care you'll grow big and strong, my little son."

C. H. A.

The Dew

Old Lazar was hoeing the garden beds before the sun was up. The dawn's rays were lifting the sun onto the earth as Lazar shook his grey head of hair, leaned on the hoe and smiled, for he dearly loved such a glimmering twilight. Imaginatively, he always painted the future of his children, grandchildren and great-grandchildren in the indistinct light of the dawn.

All is peaceful. The birds sing, and the dew stings his bare feet. But every blade of grass endures this burden of dew gladly, as if it were a heaven-sent potion.

"Ah, dew! You have been stinging me since I was a child. I often cried because of you as I herded sheep, and when I was a youth, I had to turn up the pant-legs of my white trousers when returning from my girl's, so that mother wouldn't scold me. When I became a propertied peasant and went out to cut the grain, you bit at my feet and gnawed them, defending every blade from the scythe, so that you might water it again the following morning with your bracing drink. But in the autumn you are at your worst, for all these things whose faces you washed every day are then taken away from you. You are like a mother refusing to surrender her children.

"Many a time have I walked on you, dew, and you have stung me much too much. But your sting has been as honey, nippy, but pleasant to the taste. I haven't passed you up for seventy years, not even for a single day, as I sought the bright sun, so that, in its greatness and kindness, it might dry me, and take you, dew, up to the skies from where you were to be sprayed again on all living things that wither and wane in the evening. You, O God, water the whole earth with dew as we water a hot-bed. O you precious heavenly fluid, you have given health and strength to the wheat and rye, but I, too, have been nipped and made strong by you. It grieves me much that you are not able to moisten me when you, blessed sun, begin to rise and are born again."

He looked at his whitewashed cottage.

"And how quietly do I go out of you, my palace, so as not to awaken my grandchildren who sleep in heaps. Sprawled out, they sleep so peacefully, it would be a sin to have the door squeak. Their sleep is sacred because God has taken and placed them on His lap, and on His holy lap they grow. My wife rises after I do, covers the children and walks softly as a cat, preparing their breakfast. My gracious God, how can I repay Your goodness? With Your sun and wind and rain You have sustained my strength these many years, so that my children and their children might live and grow.

"But our grandchildren are different than those of the days gone by. They read books and sing different songs. And my foolish old woman rejoices with them and tries to build a Ukraine. The grandchildren have turned her head and made her silly. They wheedle money out of her for the theatre, for books, and drag the old bag to the Reading Room.[1] And she returns home with them as gay as a young girl.

" 'Listen, old man,' she says, 'you should just see the kind of a cossack our Toma is, in his grey cap and blue breeches. The people just clap their hands listening to him speak to them as out of a book, with such passion that his shirt seems aflame. Oh, if you saw them but once!' Then I say to her: 'I'm too old to look at such things. And I'm not to blame if, because of your grand-children, you've become girlish again. But tell me, where do you get the money to buy fur caps, blue cloth and those flaming shirts? You've become so nutty about that Ukraine of yours, I'm always missing some money in my pouch.'

"But my grandchildren don't drink or waste their time danc-ing; they stay away from the tavern, and like bees they hum: 'Ukraine, Ukraine.' Young Kirilo[2] plays up to me as to a child: 'Grandpa, grandpa, I'll read you something nice.'

[1] A society where illiterate peasants heard books and newspapers read to them.
[2] Cyril.

"So he reads, and what is written there sounds good. But I can't read or write, and sit down beside the small boy just because he is so eager. All I can do is say, 'yes, yes.'

"They are well-behaved, may God bless them and their hopes! They want new things. And that's only right, because they're young."

He was wrested from those meditations by the sun which had risen like a golden disc, and by his old wife who was calling him to breakfast.

"Eternal Sun, again you bless me at breakfast time. I've grown weak, and your daughter, dew, can't drink anything more out of me, because I'm all bones. But I have many grandchildren. The dew has plenty of them to sprinkle with her pearls. And you, bright Sun, mother of us all, continue to bless them, too, at breakfast time."

Old Lazar wiped his moist eyes with a dewy leaf, and went into the cottage to be among his grandchildren.

The Schoolboy

In the office of the municipal house there gathered a crowd of irritated, clamorous women. Only the gendarme, with a carbine in his hands, and the reeve sat composed at the table, and on the floor, in a corner, behind the reeve, squatted a small boy,[1] all in rags, who scanned all those present with his glossy dark eyes.

"Why are you after this kid, women?"

"We want you to lock him up. There's no living in the village for us and our children because of him."

The women raised an outcry and wrung their hands.

"Come, Tofanka,[2] tell us the whole story. It was you who first rushed to the gendarme."

"Do I have to tell you more about that bastard? Out in the meadows he gets the little boys together, feeds them flies and

[1] An illegitimate child born during the war.
[2] Colloquial for Theophania.

worms. Their mouths swell up so that no one can sleep at night, they cry so hard. The children take out to him whatever they see in the house. With the gypsies he eats carrion flesh. Nothing like him has ever been seen in the world. Ever since his mother died, he's become wild. Nobody feeds him, nobody lets him in for the night, nobody washes his clothes. . . ."

From where he sat on the ground, the boy said:

"This Tofanka must be crazy. When they covered my mother with clay, who was there left to feed me and wash my clothes? Whatever I laid my hands on, I ate, and then didn't feel hungry; whatever I stole that was hanging on a fence, I put it on myself. People beat me for that, and beat me hard. But I can stand it. If mother isn't around, I have to stand it."

"Just look at him! At least if he pulled a long face, cried, or said he was sorry! But no, he's talking like a smart-aleck."

"Go ahead, Tofanka, tell us everything he did."

"Well, I saw my Lukin[3] off to school. I washed him, fed him, put a clean shirt on him, and he took his bag of books, his ink-stand, and some bread which he put inside the front side of his shirt, and away he went. I was carding the wool in front of the **house and wasn't even thinking** of anything when in an hour or so something rushed through the gate looking like the devil himself. It was painted all over with all kinds of colours and was screaming so loud that my ears were just pierced with the shrieks. Only by its voice did I recognize that it was my boy. I snatched him up into my arms, hurried into the house, washed him, beat him, making him cry all the more. As you see, my sleeves and shirt front are smeared with all kinds of paint. . . ."

The women examined the colourings on Tofanka's shirt and wondered if the paint would come off.

"The child was hoarse from crying, but told me that, as he was on his way to school, that bastard ran across the meadows to catch up with him, and said:

" 'Listen, Lukin, take off your shirt and I'll paint your skin with all the colours. The boys will run after you and have fun.' The boy took off his shirt and, as they stood near the pond, the other painted him. – 'Now run around the meadow for a while,' he told him, 'you'll feel like a butterfly.' That done, he snatched the shirt and the small sash and ran off into the cornstalks. The ugly brat then dressed himself, spilled ink over the garment, and went to school."

[3] Colloquial for Luke.

Having said that, Tofanka made a dash to get at the boy and beat him, but the gendarme saved him by stepping in front of him.

"I'm telling you that this Tofanka is crazy. Does she think that I'm afraid of her because the gendarme and the reeve are here? Even on the road I wouldn't be scared, because I can run as fast as the wind. And at the pond I'm not scared either, because I can push anybody right into it. I was caned long enough before I got wise to myself. I lost enough blood from my eyes, ears and throat before I learned what's what and before I could stand up on my two strong legs. Now I can run away from anyone."

"Good people, he's a curse on all of us. Reeve, don't just wait, do something about that urchin. Why, he's turning all our children into scamps! Just look at him wink. He's making fun of us all. And is he pleased with himself!"

"See here, boy, have you an uncle, an aunt, or any relations?"

"Sure I have. But during the funeral, when they were taking all those skirts and all kinds of cloths, they let me stay with them. After that, they beat me, chased me out and wouldn't give me anything to eat. That's why I had to steal. When it was warm, I slept in the grainfields or among the cornstalks, but when it got cold, I hid myself in the manger among the cattle. And the cattle, you know, have hot breath, and I felt warm when the animals breathed on me. The boys would bring me food, and my lady teacher gave me a jacket, such a long one. . . ."

"Go to his aunt, the one who lives at the edge of the forest. Tell her to come to this office at once."

"But what are you going to do with that bastard anyway? Punish him, lock him-up. We're not free to let our children out of the house with him around."

"Then punish me. I can stand it. Look how beaten my bottom is. Just look! The bruises from all kinds of canings and birchings have all dried up on it."

And the boy raised his shirt and showed the women his naked skin.

"Just imagine! He has no shame, no modesty!" the women cried out.

"There comes his aunt."

At that moment the little boy crawled between the gendarme's legs.

"Oh, gendarme, sir! This aunt will beat me. This one beats very hard. I see everything that goes on in the village, and somehow I noticed that that fellow Bassko came to visit her once in a while. So when she heard me say that to somebody, she ran after me far out into the hayfield and hit me with something so sharp that it tore a piece of my flesh out. This one would kill me. Because women get more angry about people knowing that some man comes to see them than about anything else. I got enough caning for that, and the worst came from this aunt. They don't beat me so hard when I steal a shirt or the salted pork from them, as they do for this sort of thing."

All the women turned to the little boy's aunt and began to whisper among themselves smirkingly.

"Gendarme, sir! I know where everything is in the village. I know where the salted pork is; I know where the carbines are buried; I know where the Jew hides his watch. Because no one lets me inside, I have to walk around and look for such things myself. You can even string me up for that. I saw Les[4] hang his boy feet up. Afterwards there were so many gendarmes, and a doctor who cut him open. But in the end he was buried nicely. . . . Only don't let this aunt get me, because she's very sore about that Bassko thing. If I must go to prison, to prison I'll go; if it's the gallows for me, then that's it. But you must understand that I have to do the best I can for myself. . . ."

C. H. A.

---

[4] Colloquial for Oles, Alexander.